# JOHNNY BOO AND THE SILLY BLIZZARD

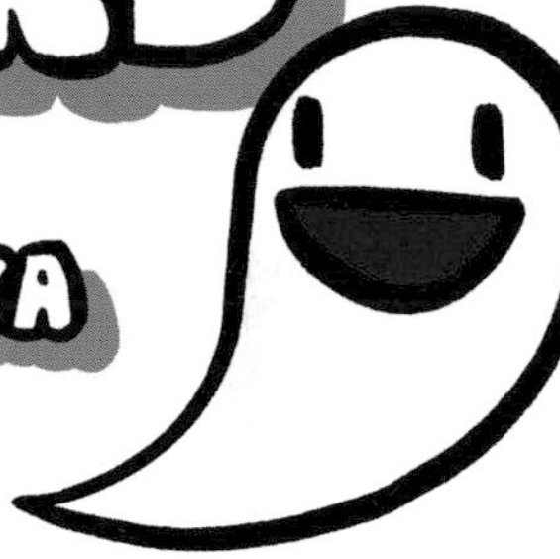

JAMES KOCHALKA

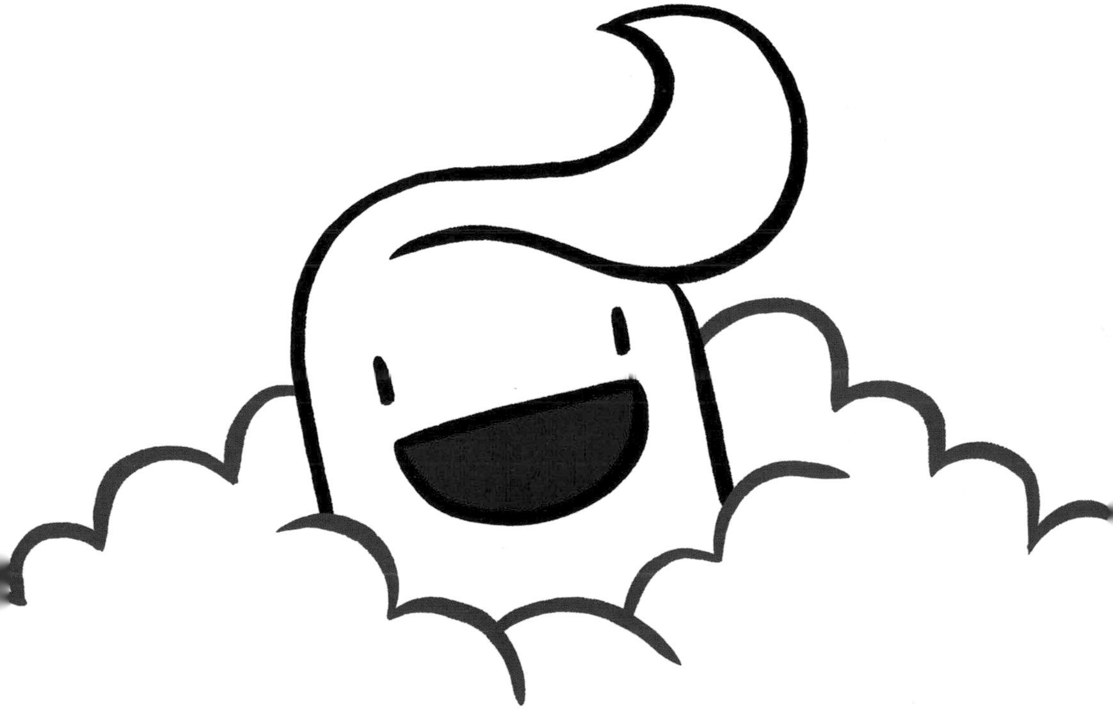

TOP SHELF PRODUCTIONS

Published by Top Shelf Productions, an imprint of IDW Publishing, a division of Idea and Design Works, LLC. Offices: Top Shelf Productions, c/o Idea & Design Works, LLC, 2765 Truxtun Road, San Diego, CA 92106. Top Shelf Productions®, the Top Shelf logo, Idea and Design Works®, and the IDW logo are registered trademarks of Idea and Design Works, LLC. All Rights Reserved. With the exception of small excerpts of artwork used for review purposes, none of the contents of this publication may be reprinted without the permission of IDW Publishing. IDW Publishing does not read or accept unsolicited submissions of ideas, stories, or artwork.

Editor-in-Chief: Chris Staros.

Edited by Leigh Walton.

Designed by Tara McCrillis.

Visit our online catalog at www.topshelfcomix.com.

Printed in China.

ISBN 978-1-60309-485-6          24 23 22 21    4 3 2 1

CHAPTER ONE

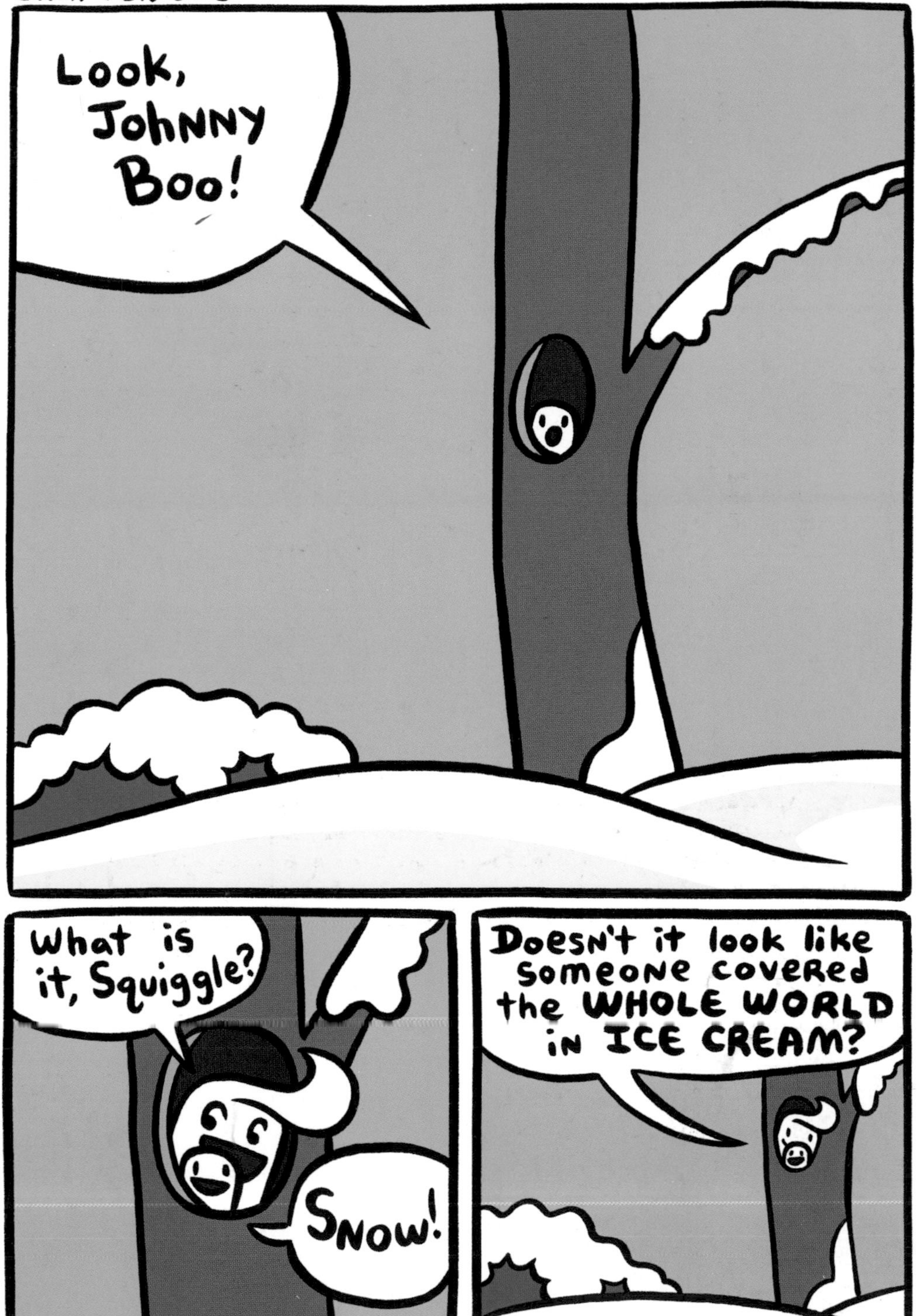
Look, Johnny Boo!
What is it, Squiggle?
Snow!
Doesn't it look like someone covered the WHOLE WORLD in ICE CREAM?

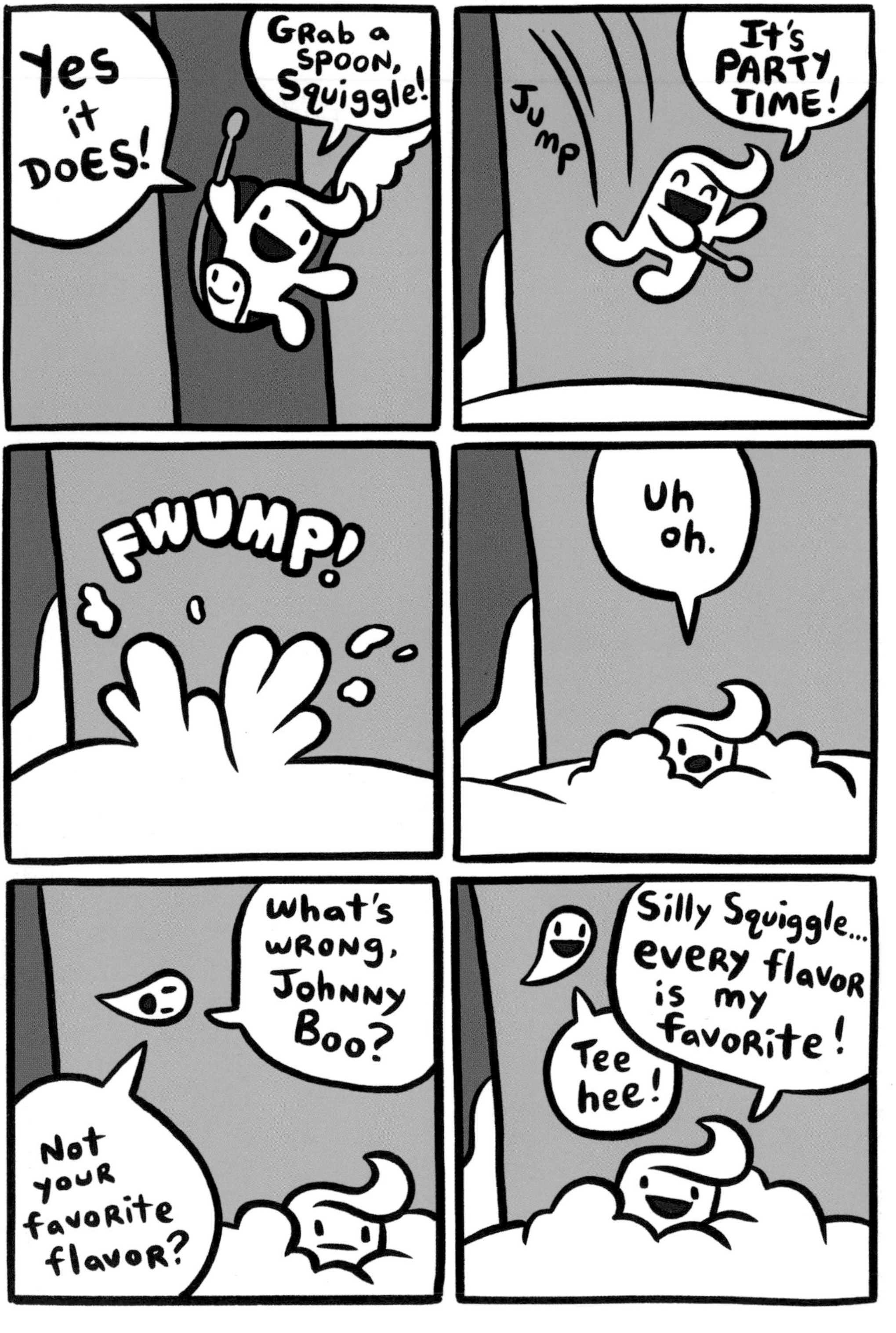
Yes it DOES!
Grab a SPOON, Squiggle!
JUMP
It's PARTY TIME!
FWUMP!
Uh oh.
What's wrong, Johnny Boo?
Not your favorite flavor?
Silly Squiggle... every flavor is my favorite!
Tee hee!

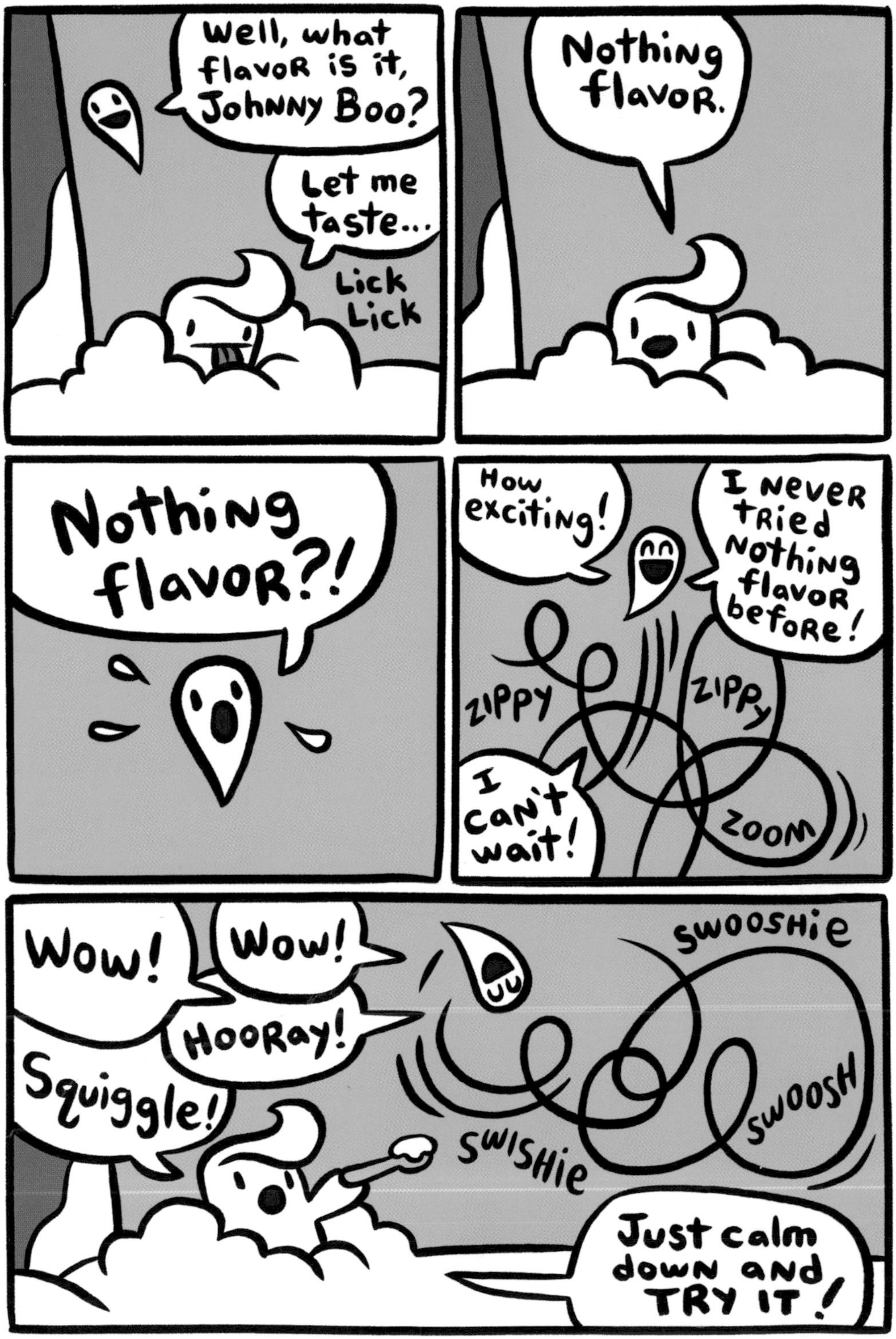
Well, what flavor is it, Johnny Boo?
Let me taste...
Lick Lick
Nothing flavor.
Nothing flavor?!
How exciting!
I never tried nothing flavor before!
ZIPPY
ZIPPY
I can't wait!
ZOOM
Wow!
Wow!
HOORAY!
Squiggle!
SWOOSHIE
SWOOSH
SWISHIE
Just calm down and TRY IT!

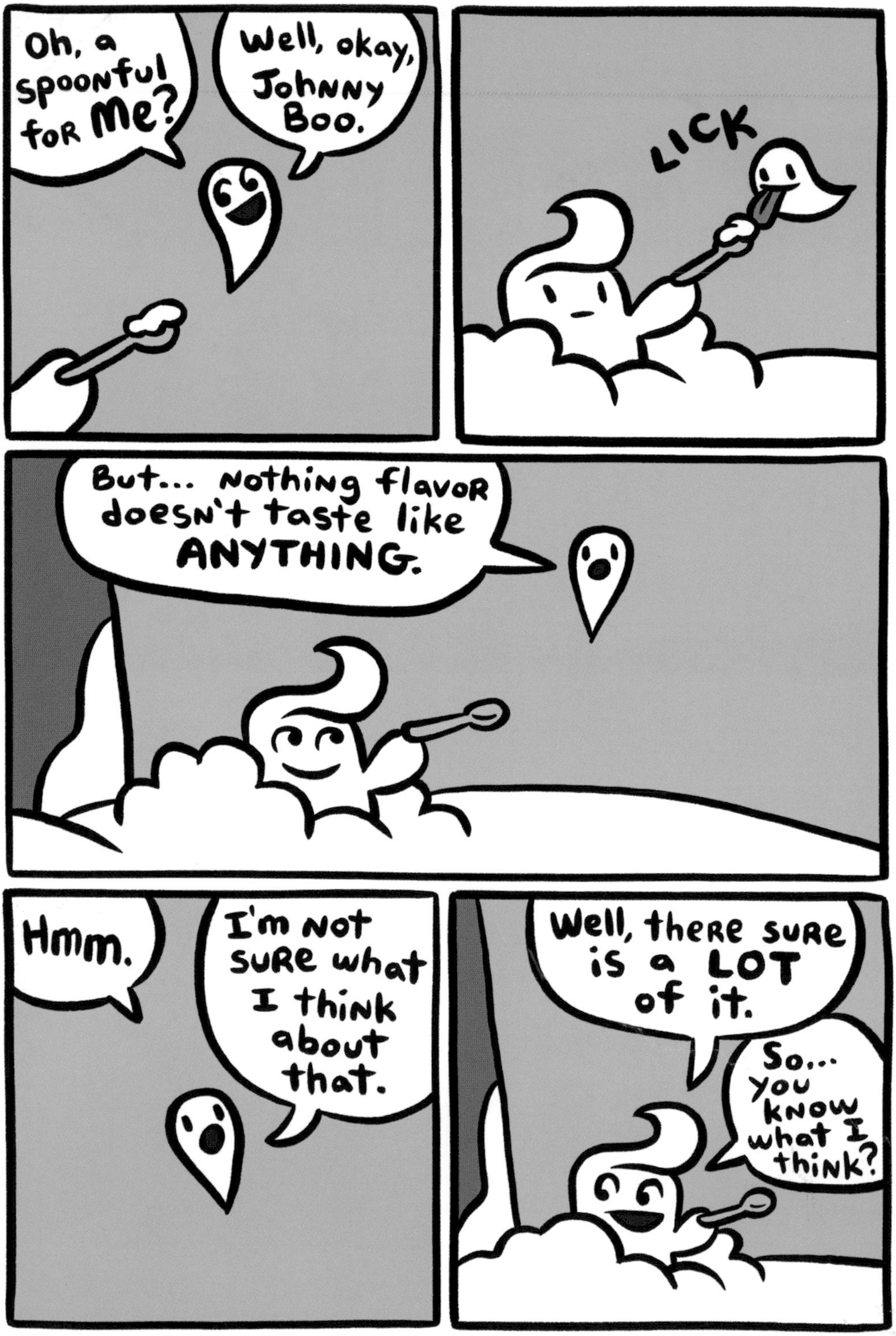
Oh, a spoonful for Me?
Well, okay, Johnny Boo.
LICK
But... Nothing flavor doesn't taste like ANYTHING.
Hmm.
I'm not sure what I think about that.
Well, there sure is a LOT of it.
So... you know what I think?

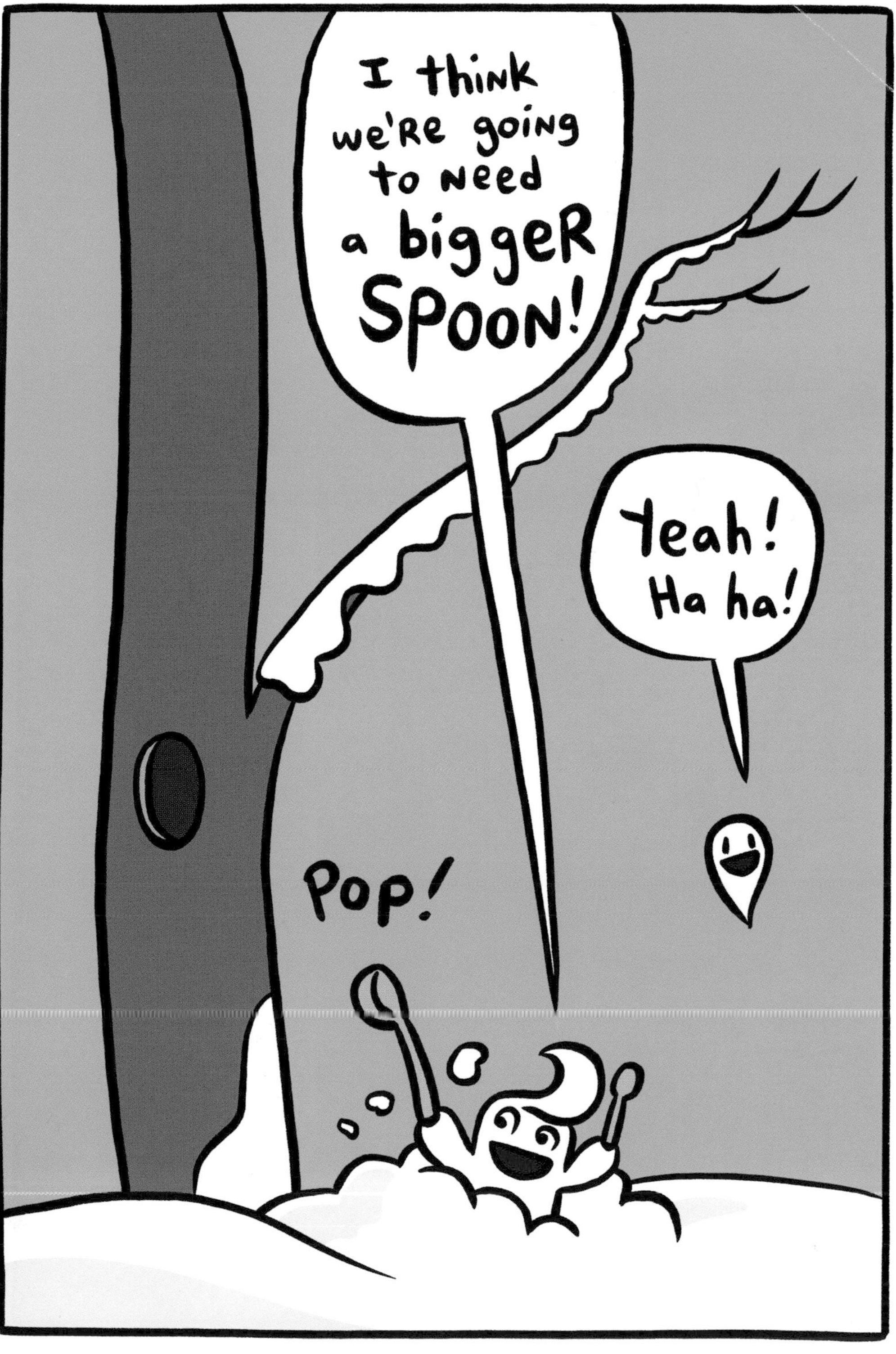
I think we're going to need a bigger SPOON!
Yeah! Ha ha!
Pop!

CHAPTER TWO

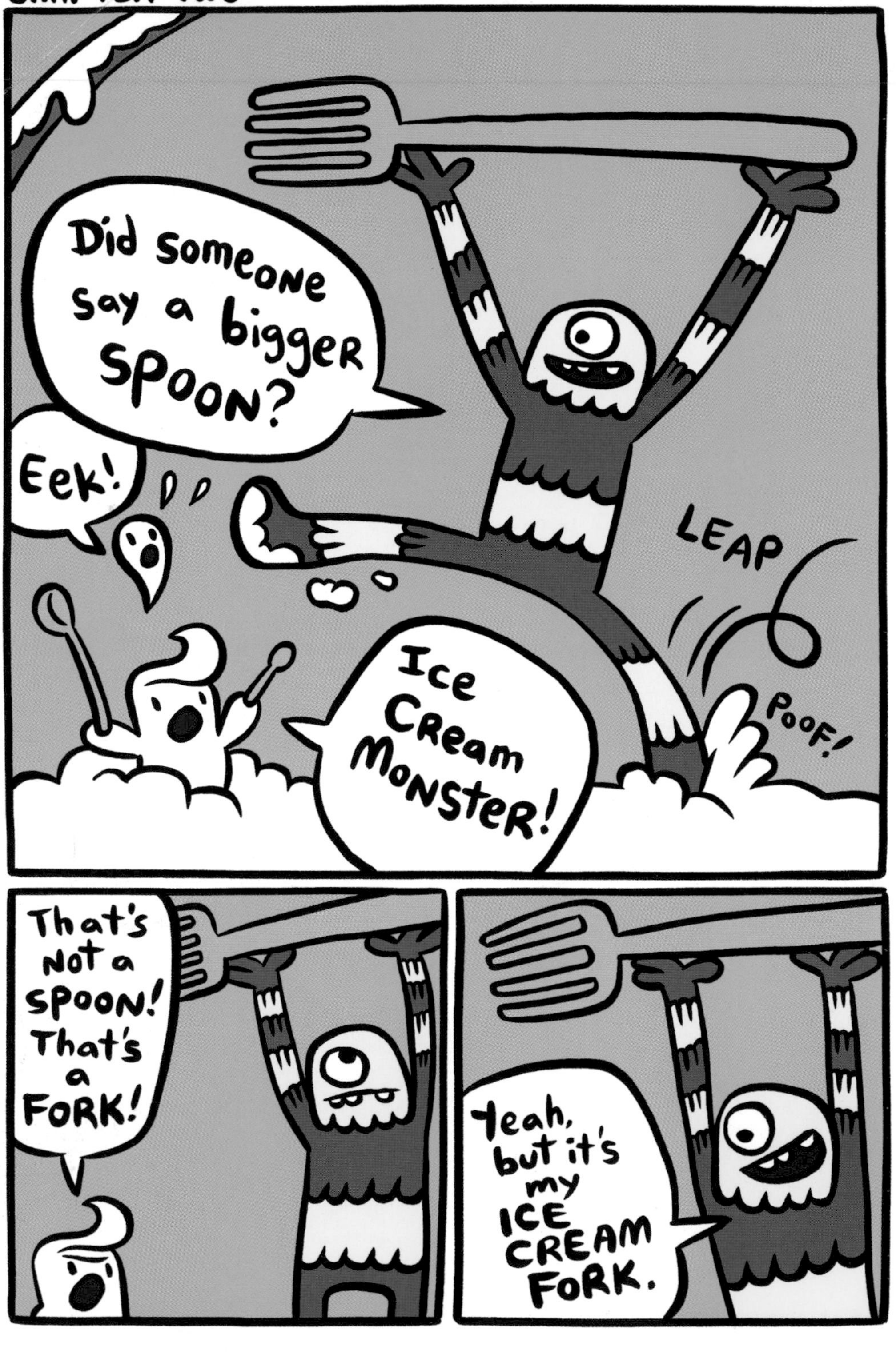
Did someone say a bigger SPOON?
Eek!
LEAP
Ice Cream Monster!
POOF!
That's Not a SPOON! That's a FORK!
Yeah, but it's my ICE CREAM FORK.

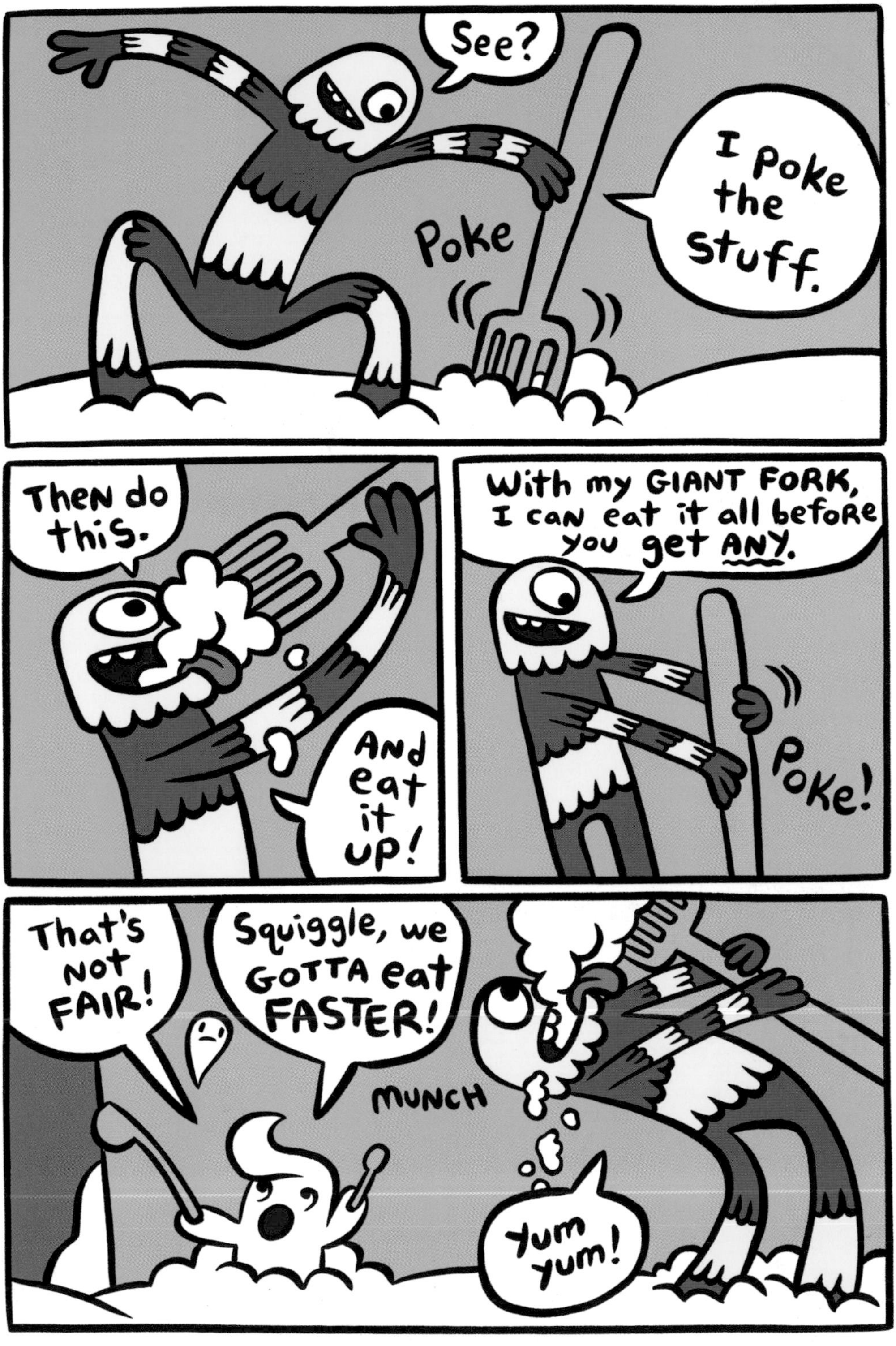
See?
I poke the stuff.
Poke
Then do this.
And eat it up!
With my GIANT FORK, I can eat it all before you get ANY.
Poke!
That's not FAIR!
Squiggle, we GOTTA eat FASTER!
MUNCH
Yum yum!

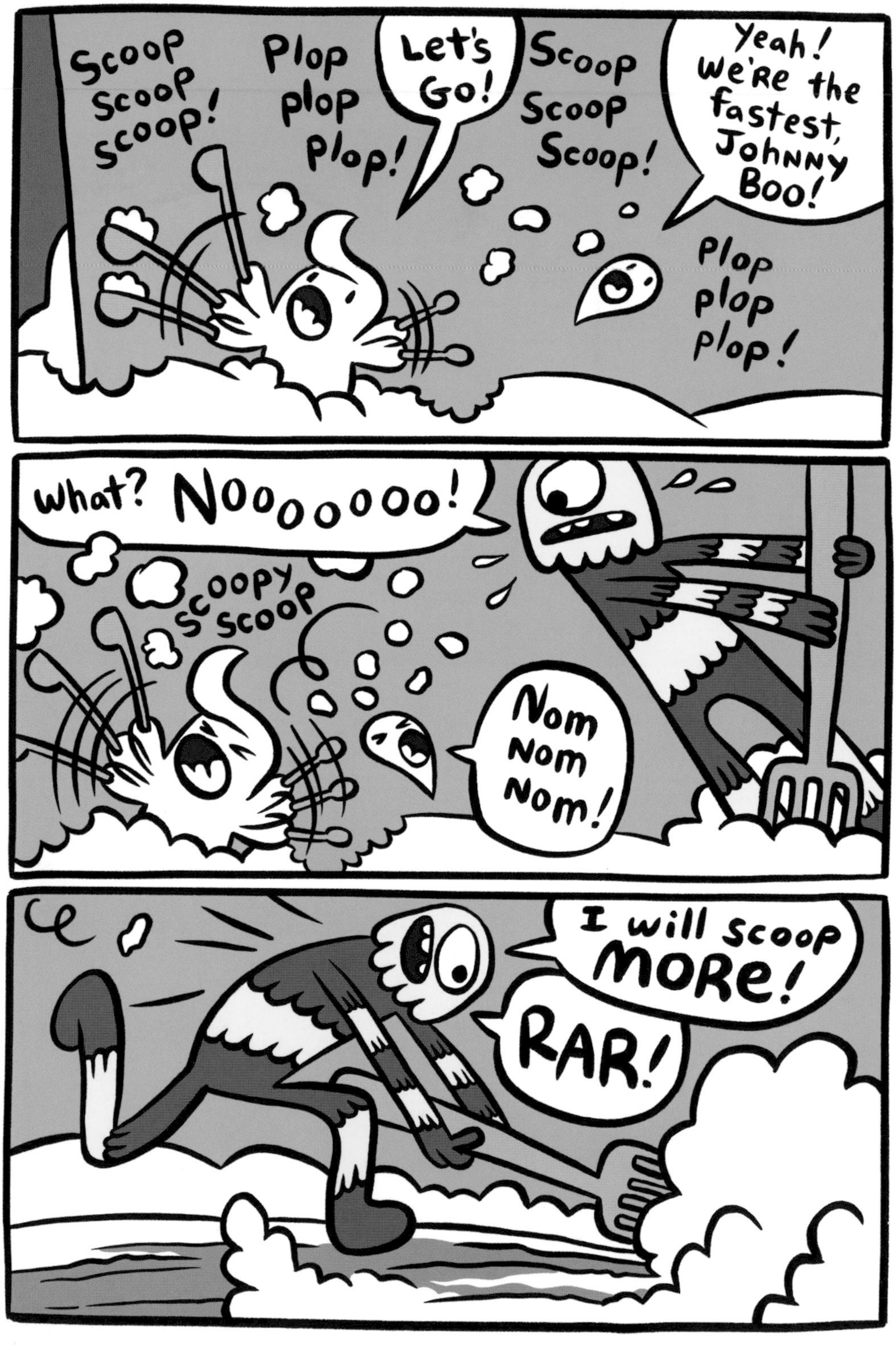
Scoop scoop scoop!
Plop plop plop!
Let's Go!
Scoop Scoop Scoop!
Yeah! We're the fastest, Johnny Boo!
Plop plop plop!
What? Nooooooooo!
Scoopy scoop
Nom Nom Nom!
I will scoop MORE!
RAR!

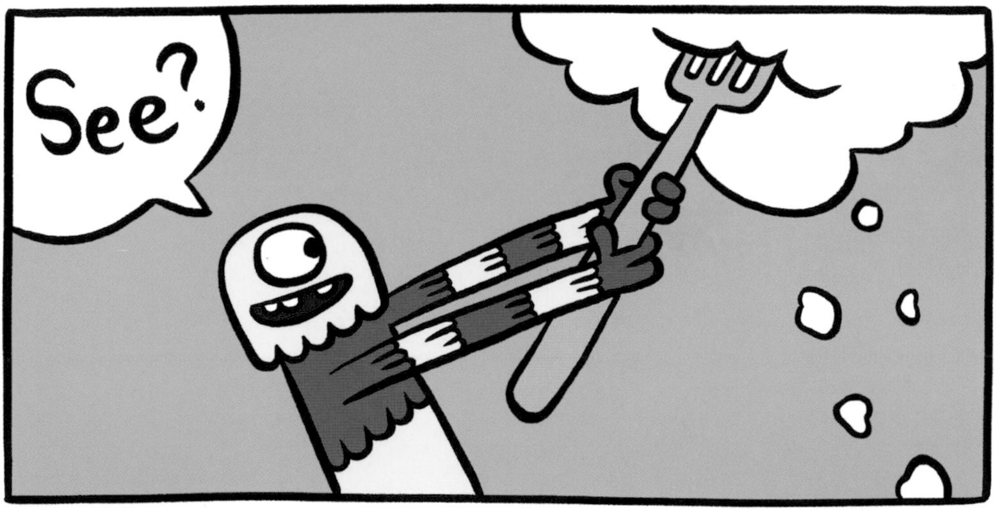
See?

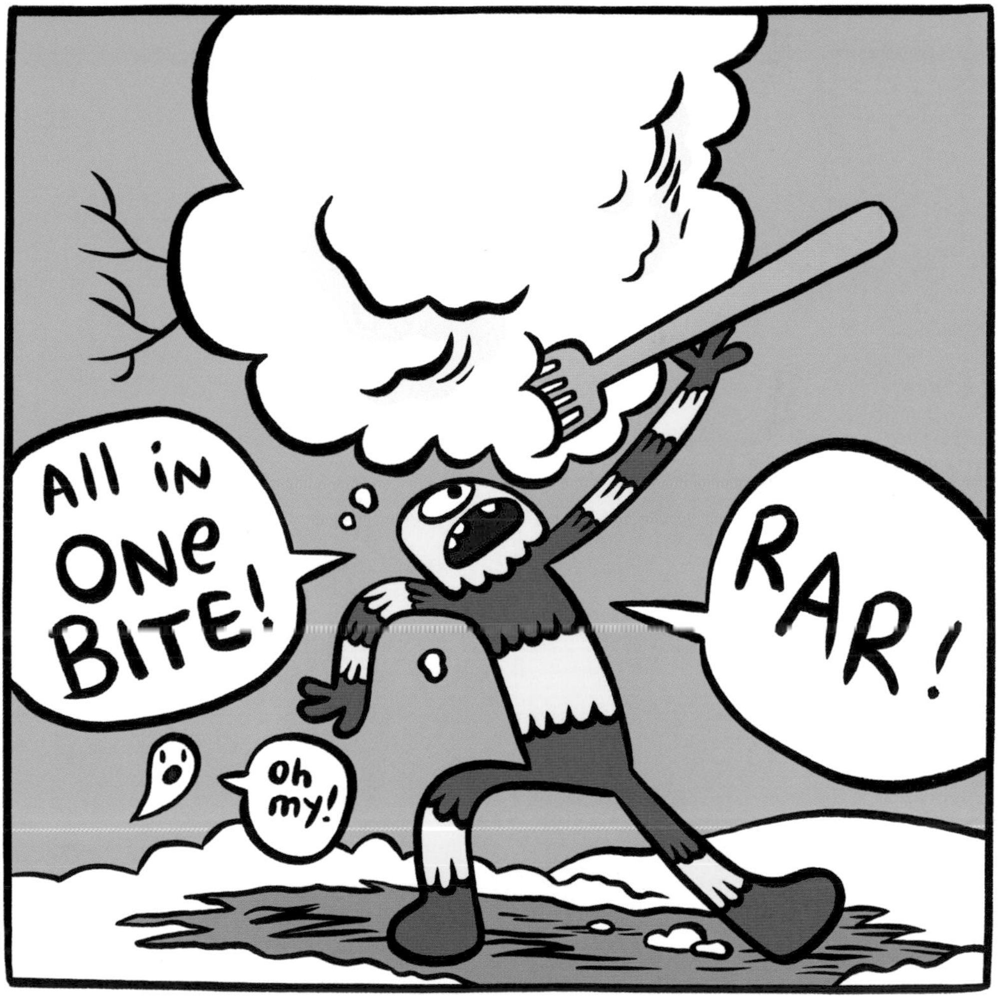
All in ONE BITE!
RAR!
oh my!

CHAPTER THREE

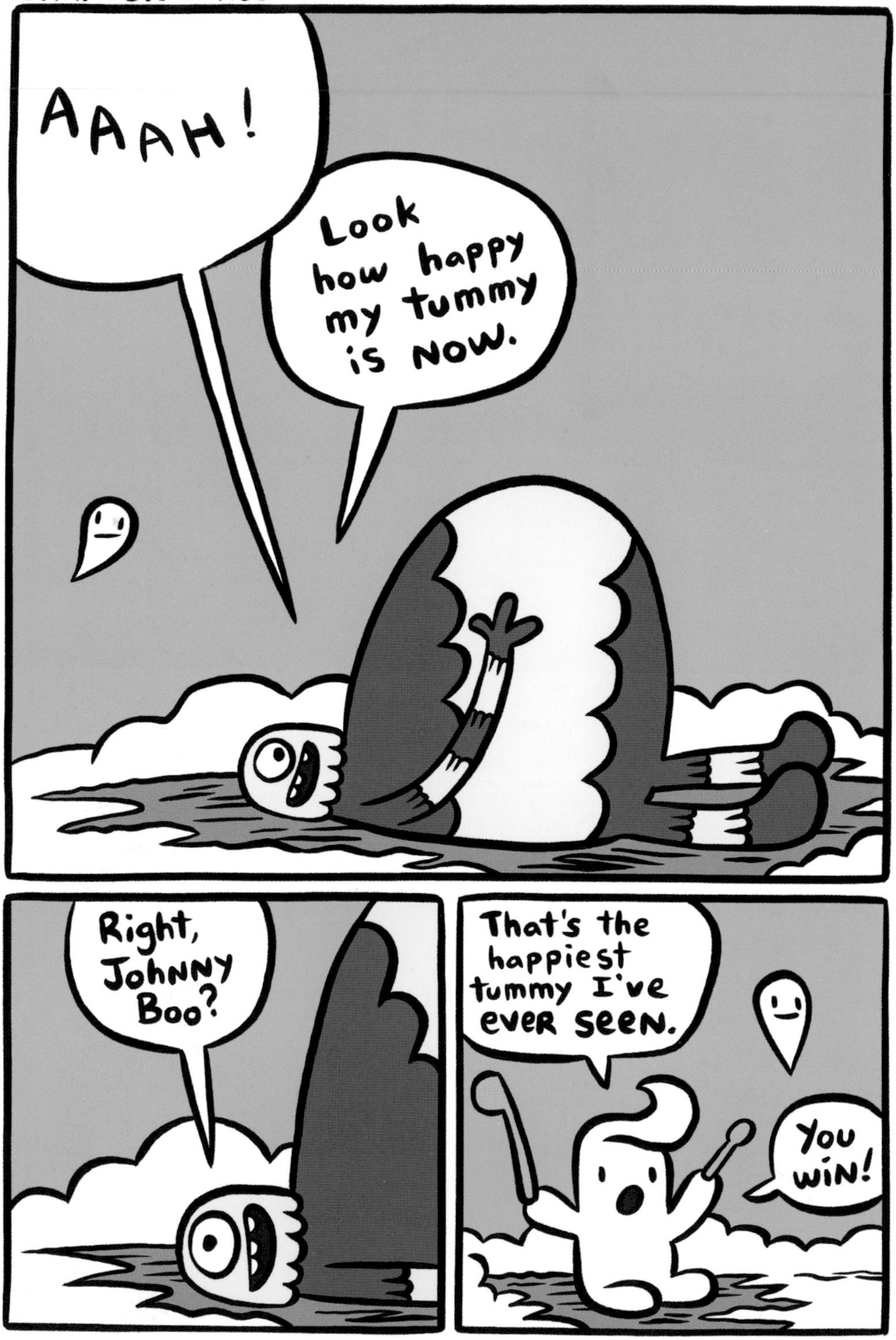
AAAH!
Look how happy my tummy is NOW.
Right, JohNNy Boo?
That's the happiest tummy I've ever seen.
You win!

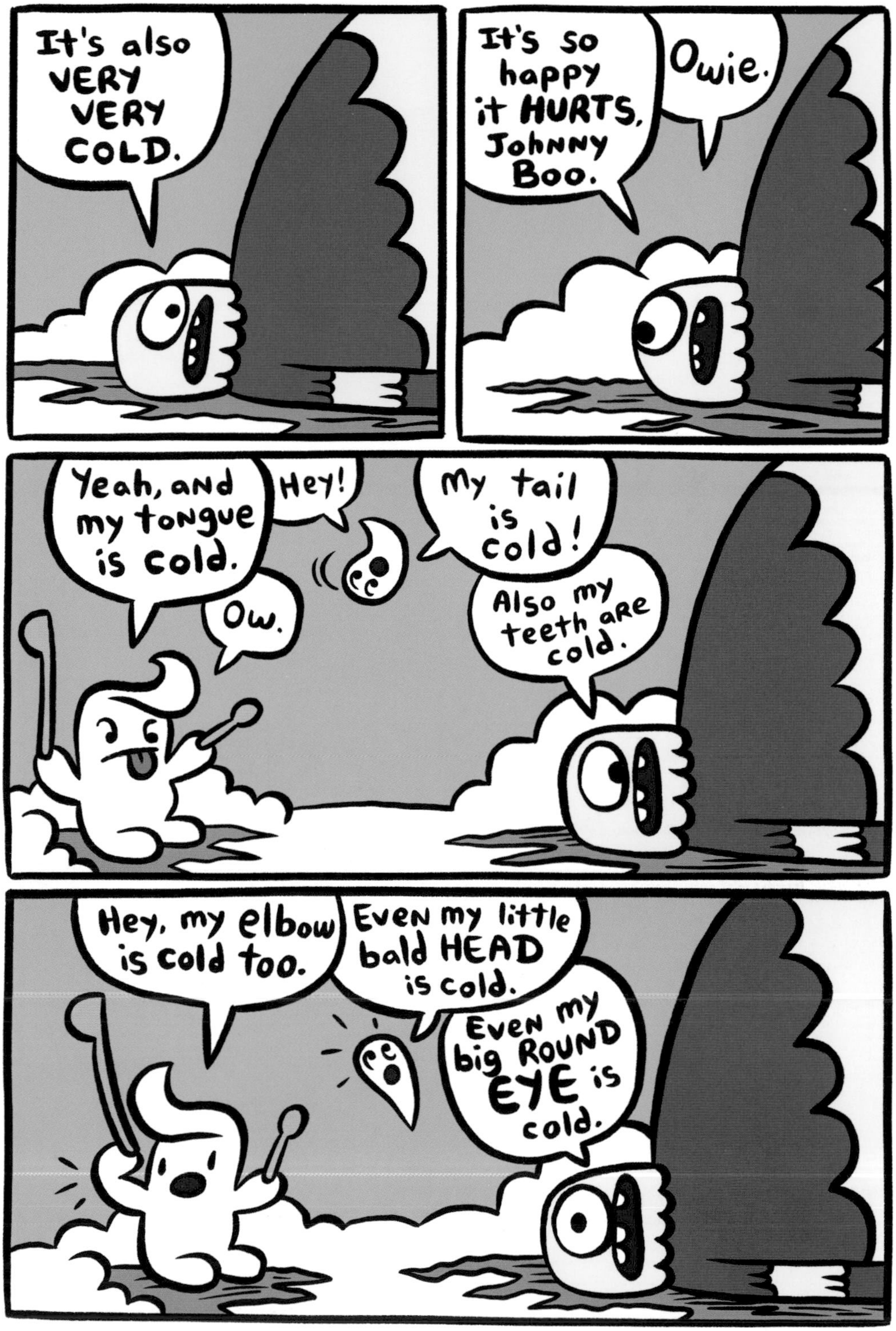
It's also VERY VERY COLD.
It's so happy it HURTS, Johnny Boo.
Owie.
Yeah, and my tongue is cold.
Hey!
My tail is cold!
Ow.
Also my teeth are cold.
Hey, my elbow is cold too.
Even my little bald HEAD is cold.
Even my big ROUND EYE is cold.

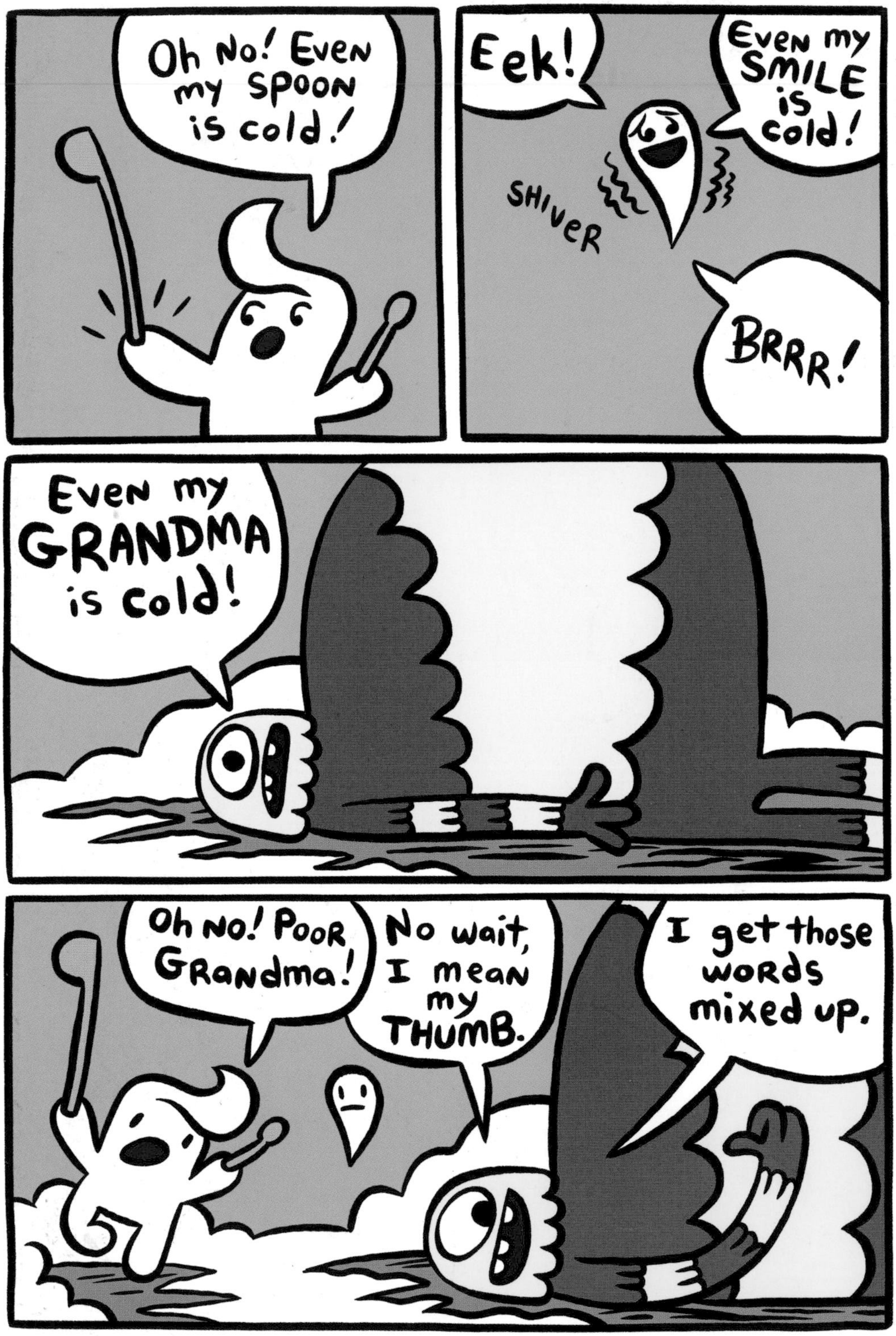

Oh No! Even my SPOON is cold!
Eek!
Even my SMILE is cold!
SHIVER
BRRR!
Even my GRANDMA is cold!
Oh No! Poor Grandma!
No wait, I mean my THUMB.
I get those words mixed up.

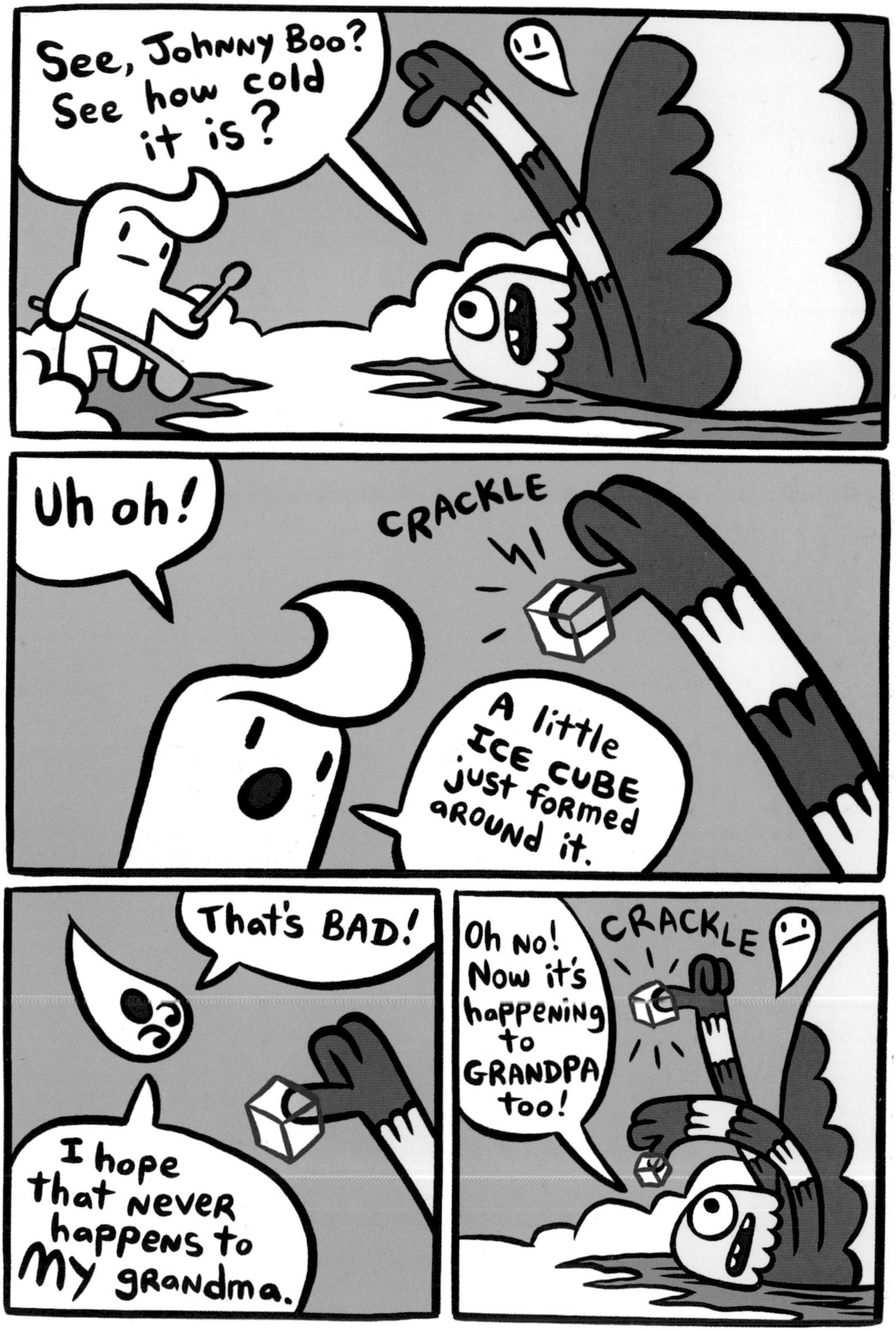

See, Johnny Boo? See how cold it is?
Uh oh!
CRACKLE
A little ICE CUBE just formed around it.
That's BAD!
I hope that NEVER happens to MY grandma.
Oh no! Now it's happening to GRANDPA too!
CRACKLE

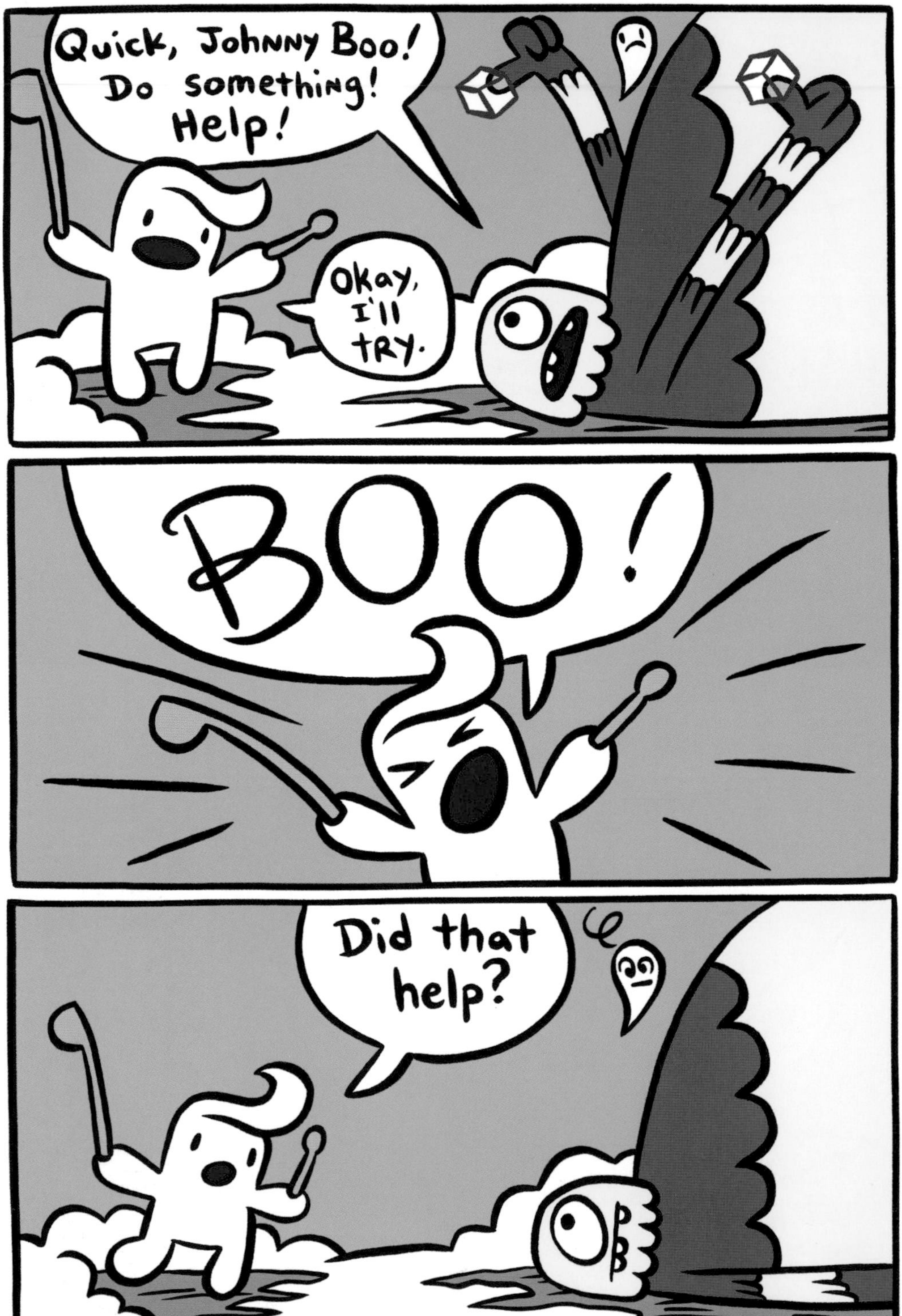
Quick, Johnny Boo! Do something! Help!
Okay, I'll try.
BOO!
Did that help?

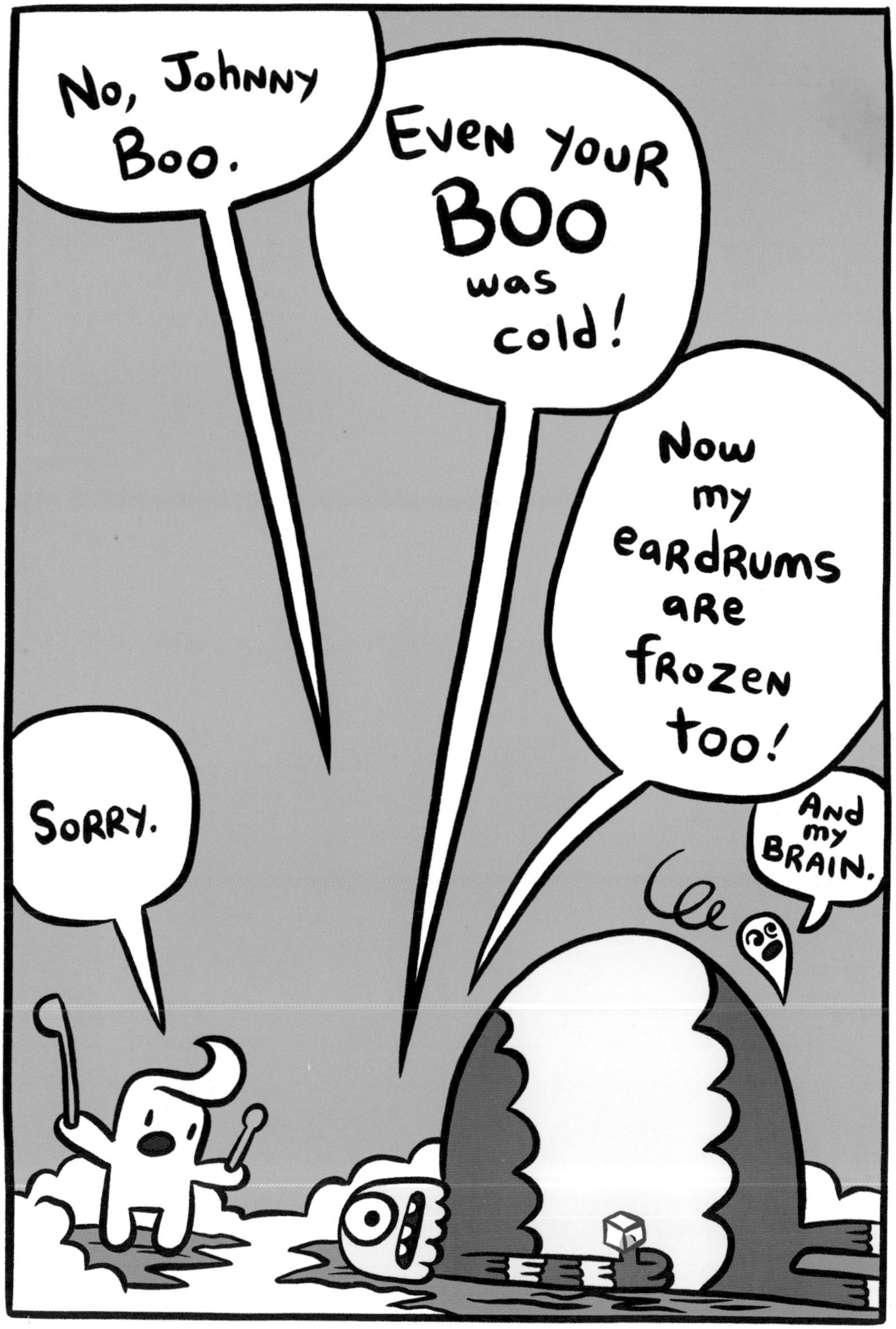
No, Johnny Boo.
Even your BOO was cold!
Now my eardrums are frozen too!
And my BRAIN.
Sorry.

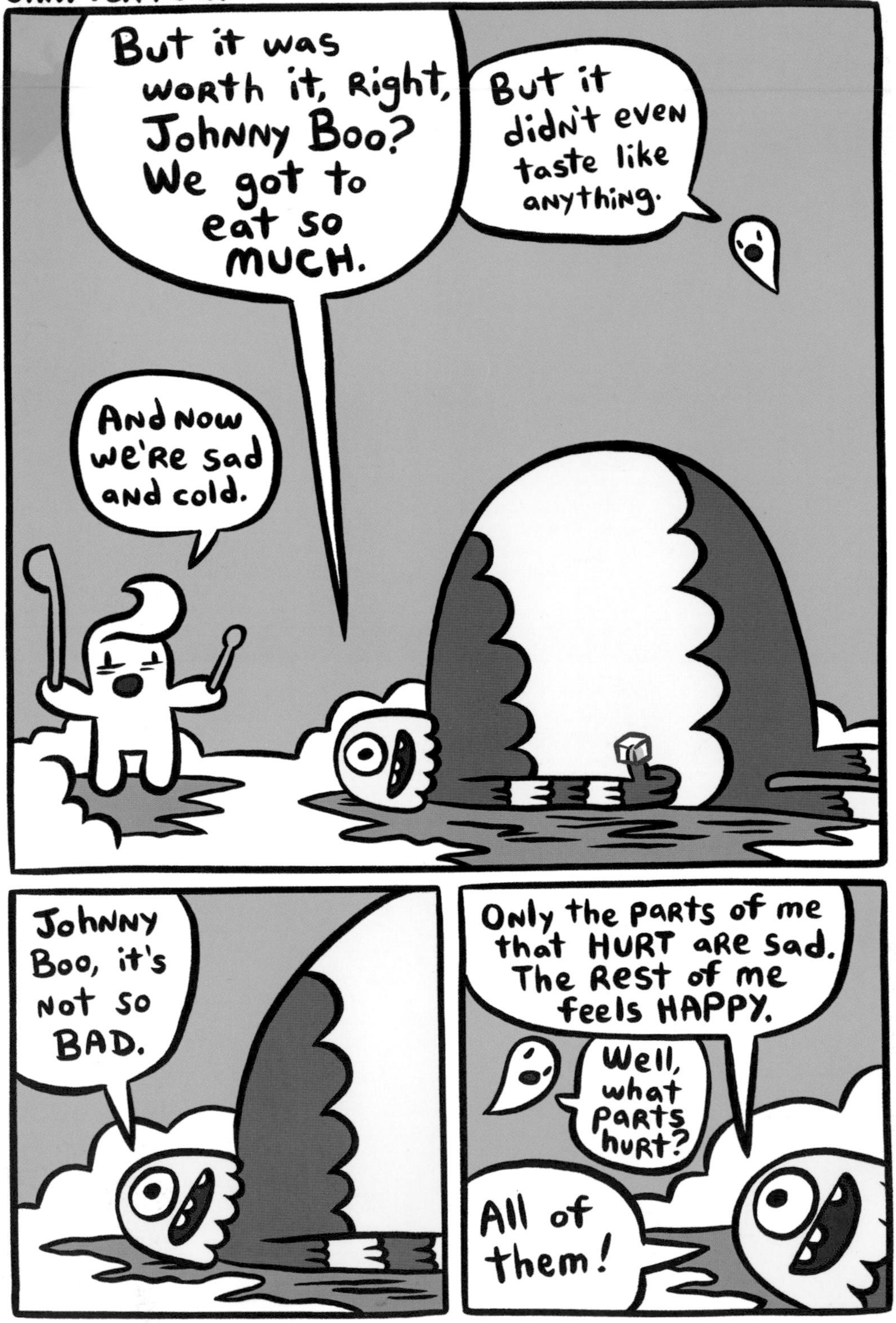
But it was worth it, right, Johnny Boo? We got to eat so MUCH.
But it didn't even taste like anything.
And now we're sad and cold.
Johnny Boo, it's not so BAD.
Only the parts of me that HURT are sad. The rest of me feels HAPPY.
Well, what parts hurt?
All of them!

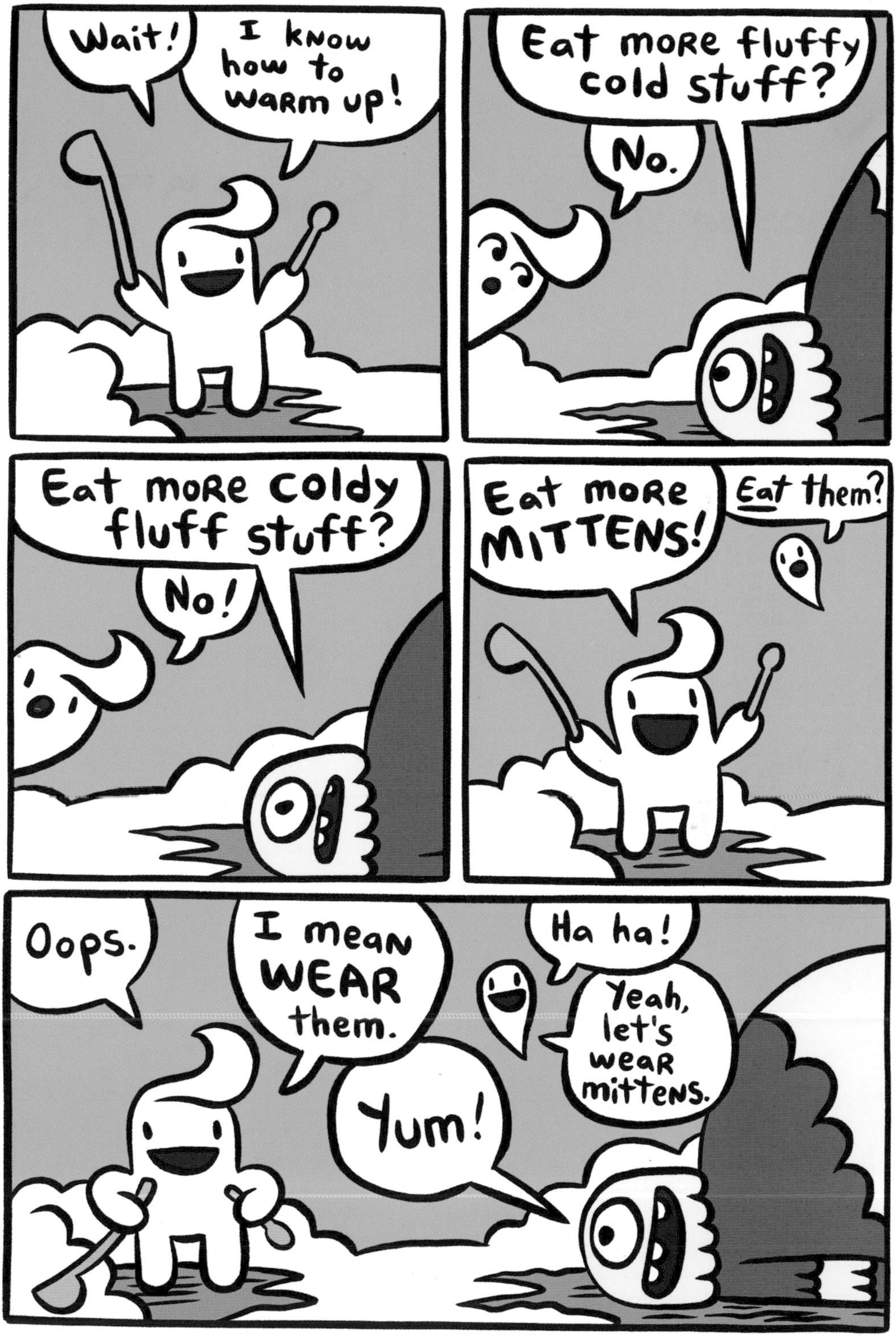
Wait!
I know how to warm up!
Eat more fluffy cold stuff?
No.
Eat more coldy fluff stuff?
No!
Eat more MITTENS!
Eat them?
Oops.
I mean WEAR them.
Yum!
Ha ha!
Yeah, let's wear mittens.

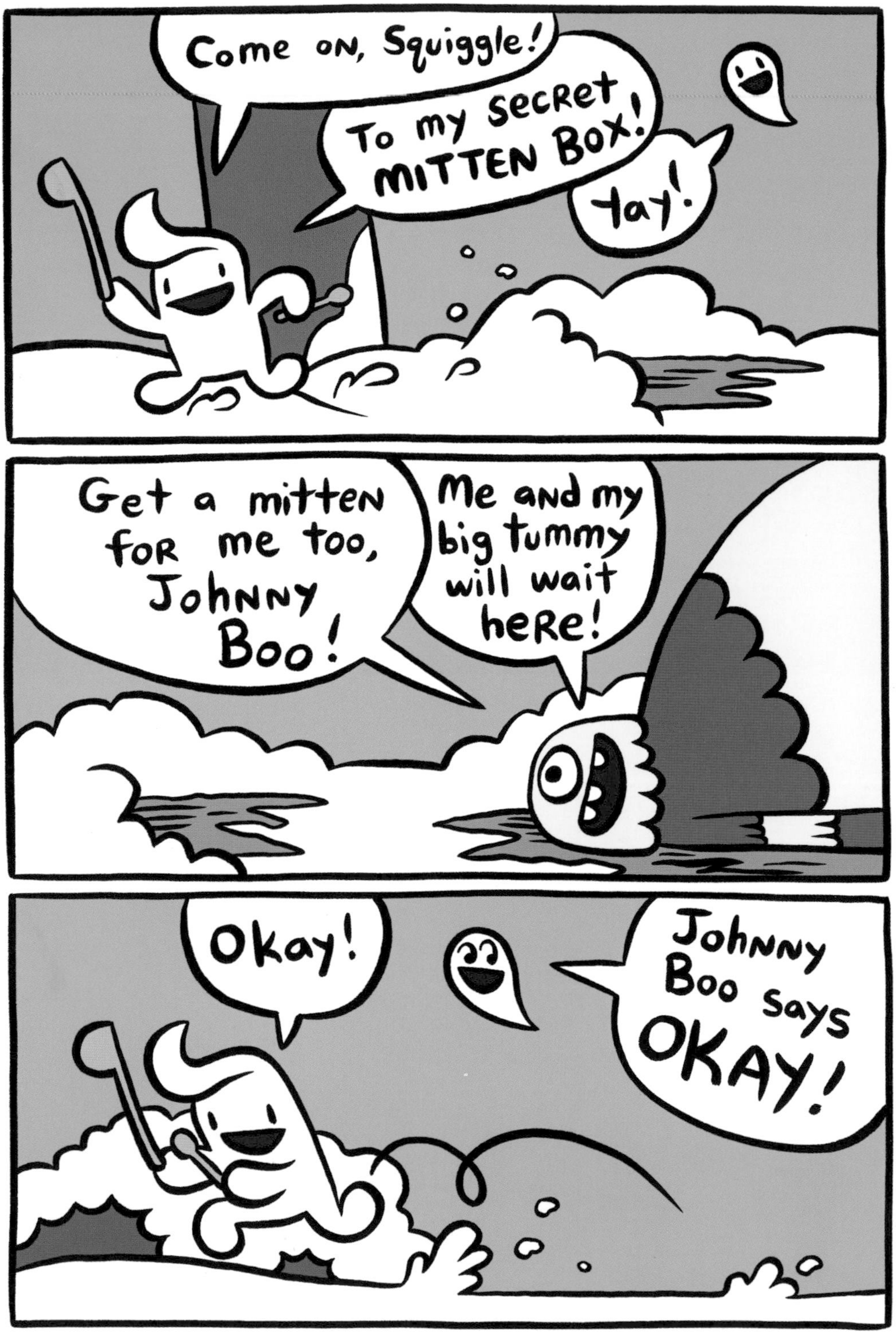
Come on, Squiggle!
To my secret MITTEN BOX!
Yay!
Get a mitten for me too, Johnny Boo!
Me and my big tummy will wait here!
Okay!
Johnny Boo says OKAY!

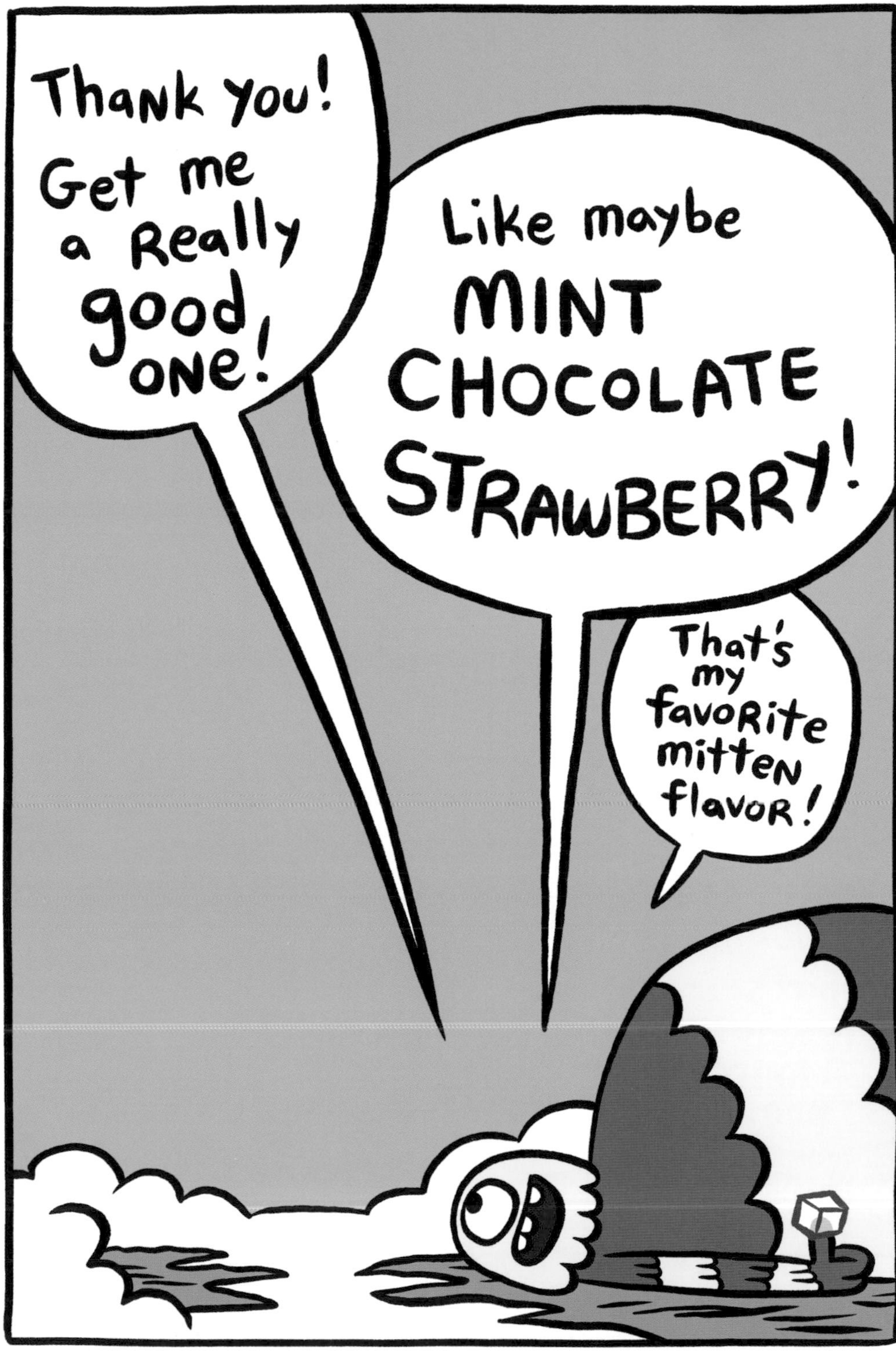
Thank you! Get me a Really good one!
Like maybe MINT CHOCOLATE STRAWBERRY!
That's my favorite mitten flavor!

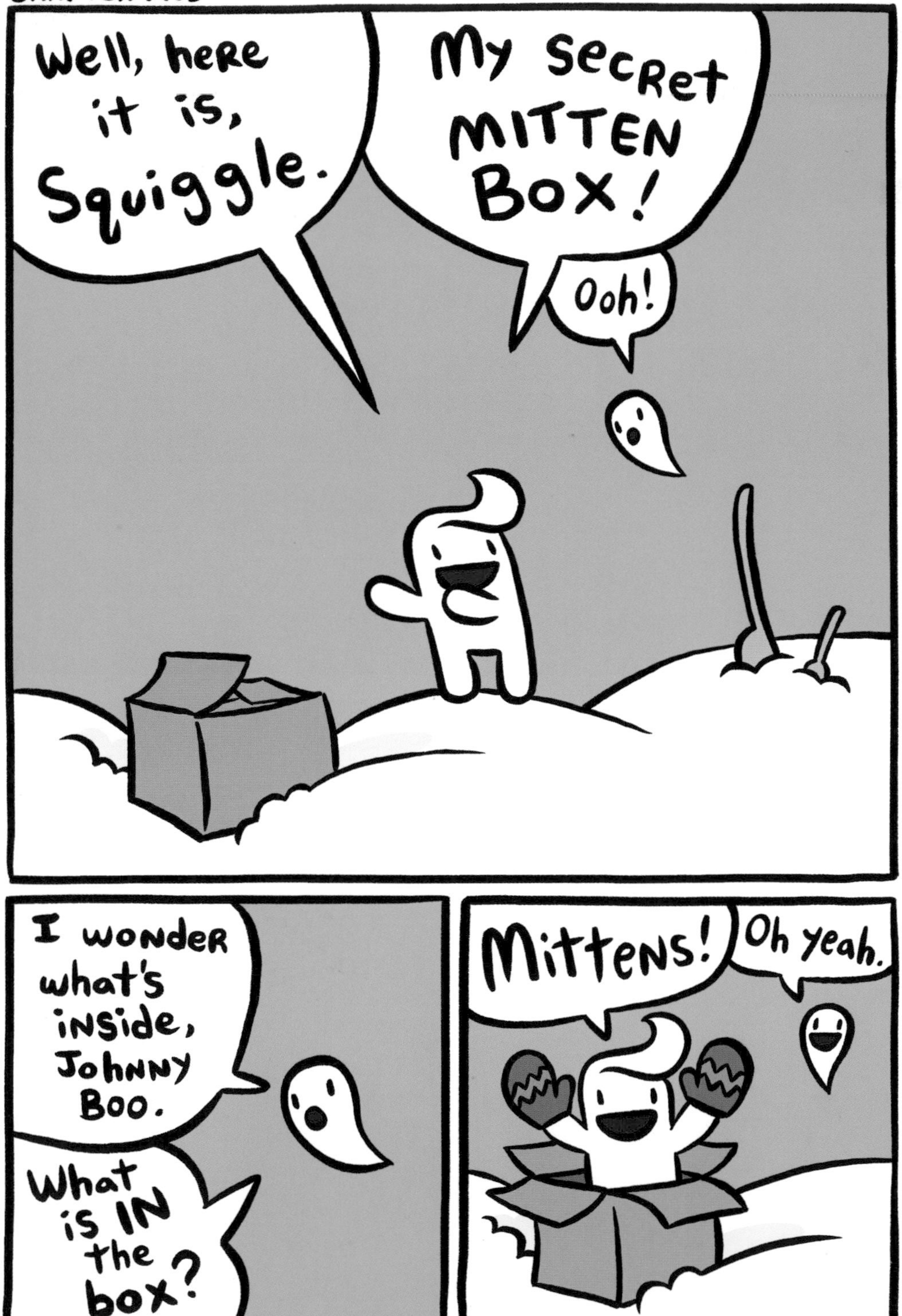
Well, here it is, Squiggle.
My secret MITTEN Box!
Ooh!
I wonder what's inside, Johnny Boo.
What is IN the box?
Mittens!
Oh yeah.

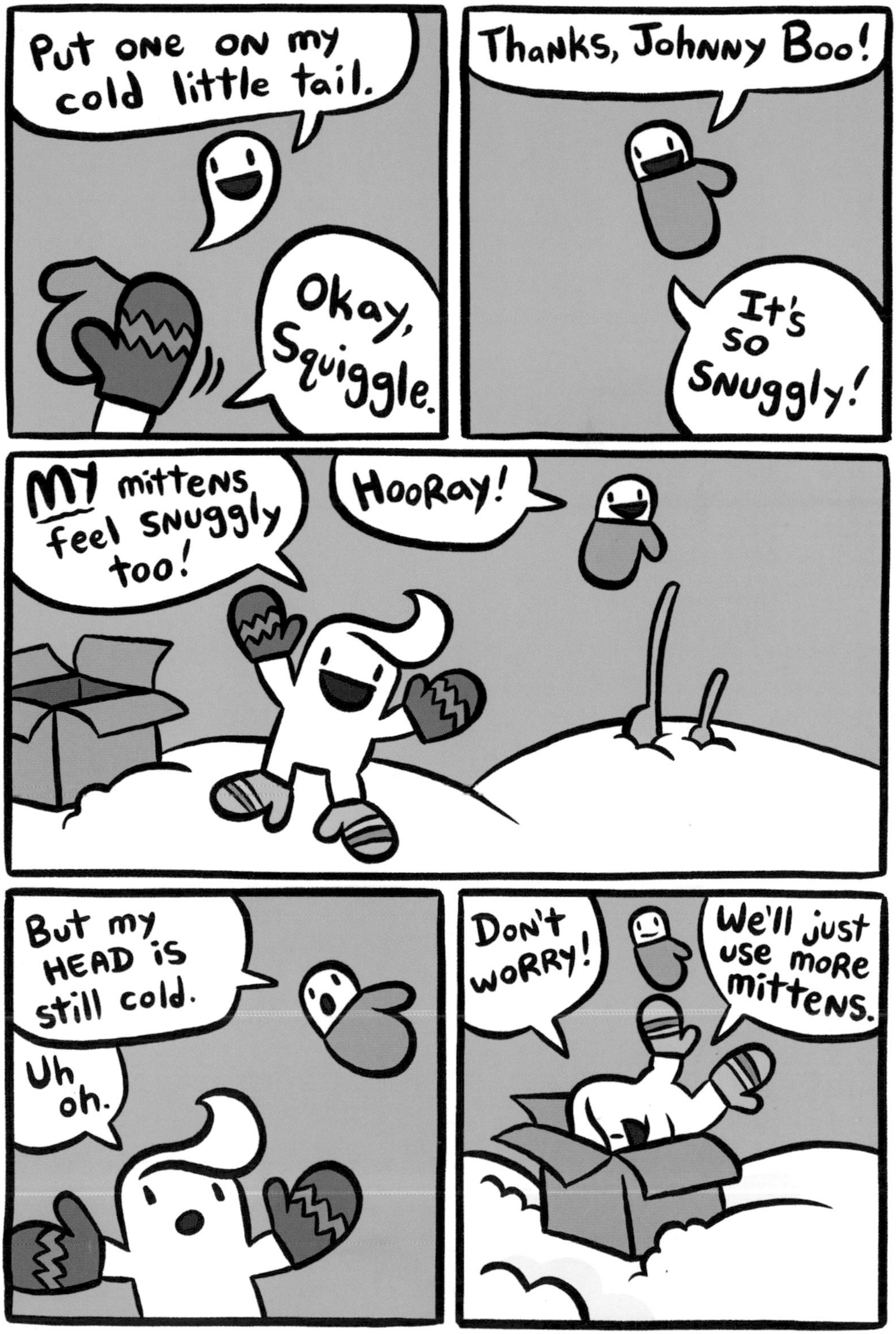
Put one on my cold little tail.
Okay, Squiggle.
Thanks, Johnny Boo!
It's so snuggly!
MY mittens feel snuggly too!
Hooray!
But my HEAD is still cold.
Uh oh.
Don't worry!
We'll just use more mittens.

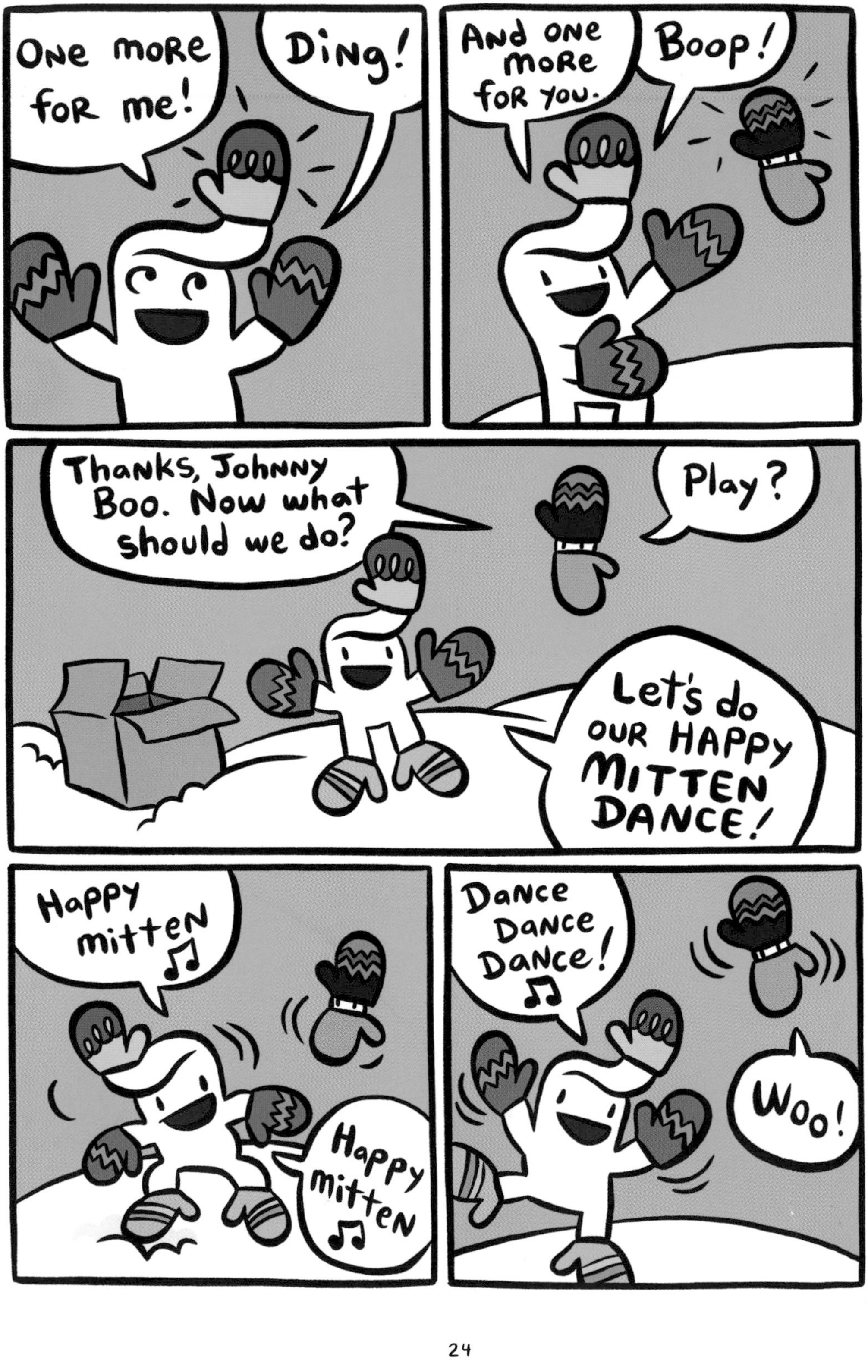
One more for me!
Ding!
And one more for you.
Boop!
Thanks, Johnny Boo. Now what should we do?
Play?
Let's do our HAPPY MITTEN DANCE!
Happy mitten ♫
Happy mitten ♫
Dance Dance Dance! ♫
Woo!

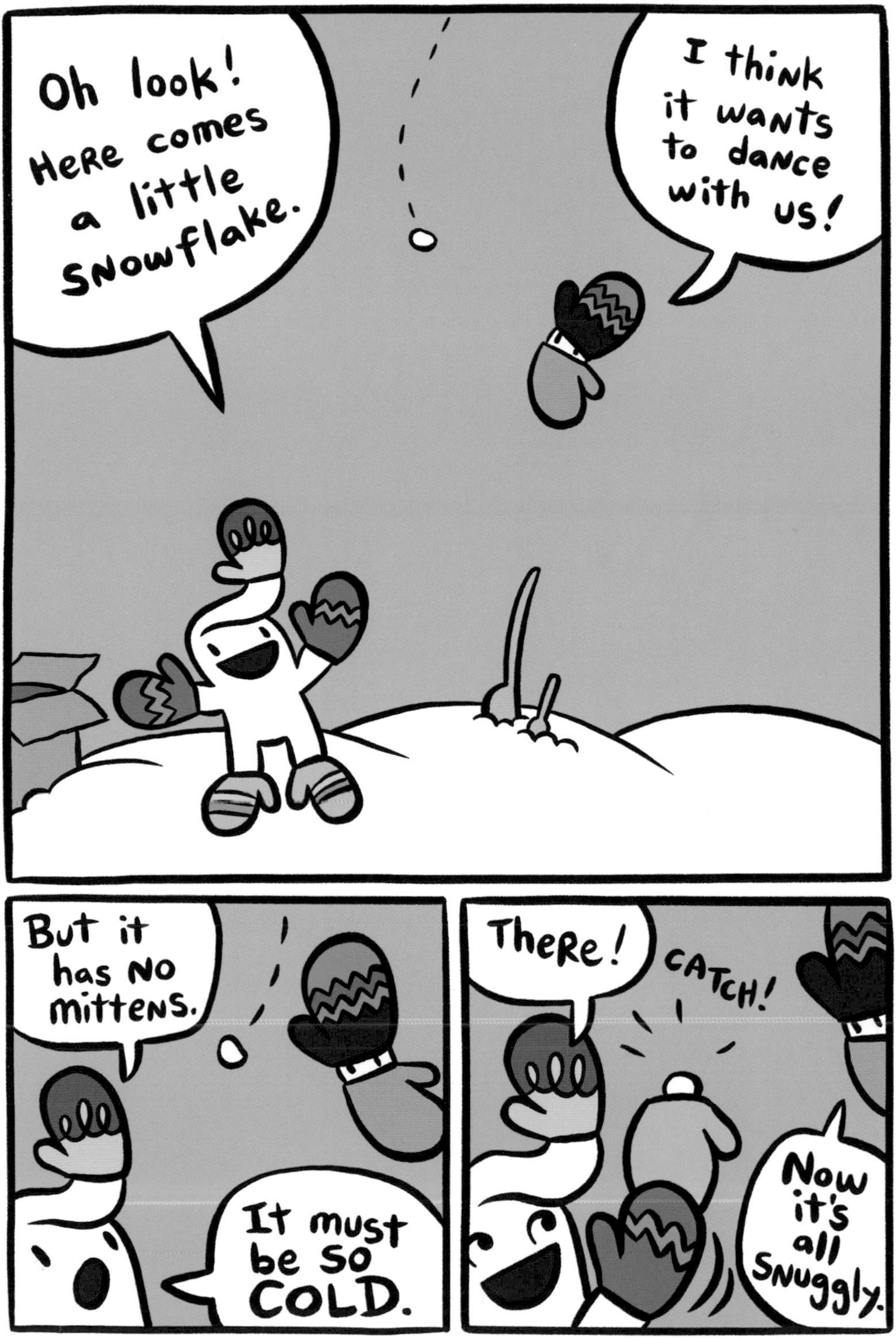
Oh look! Here comes a little snowflake.
I think it wants to dance with us!
But it has no mittens.
It must be so COLD.
There!
CATCH!
Now it's all snuggly.

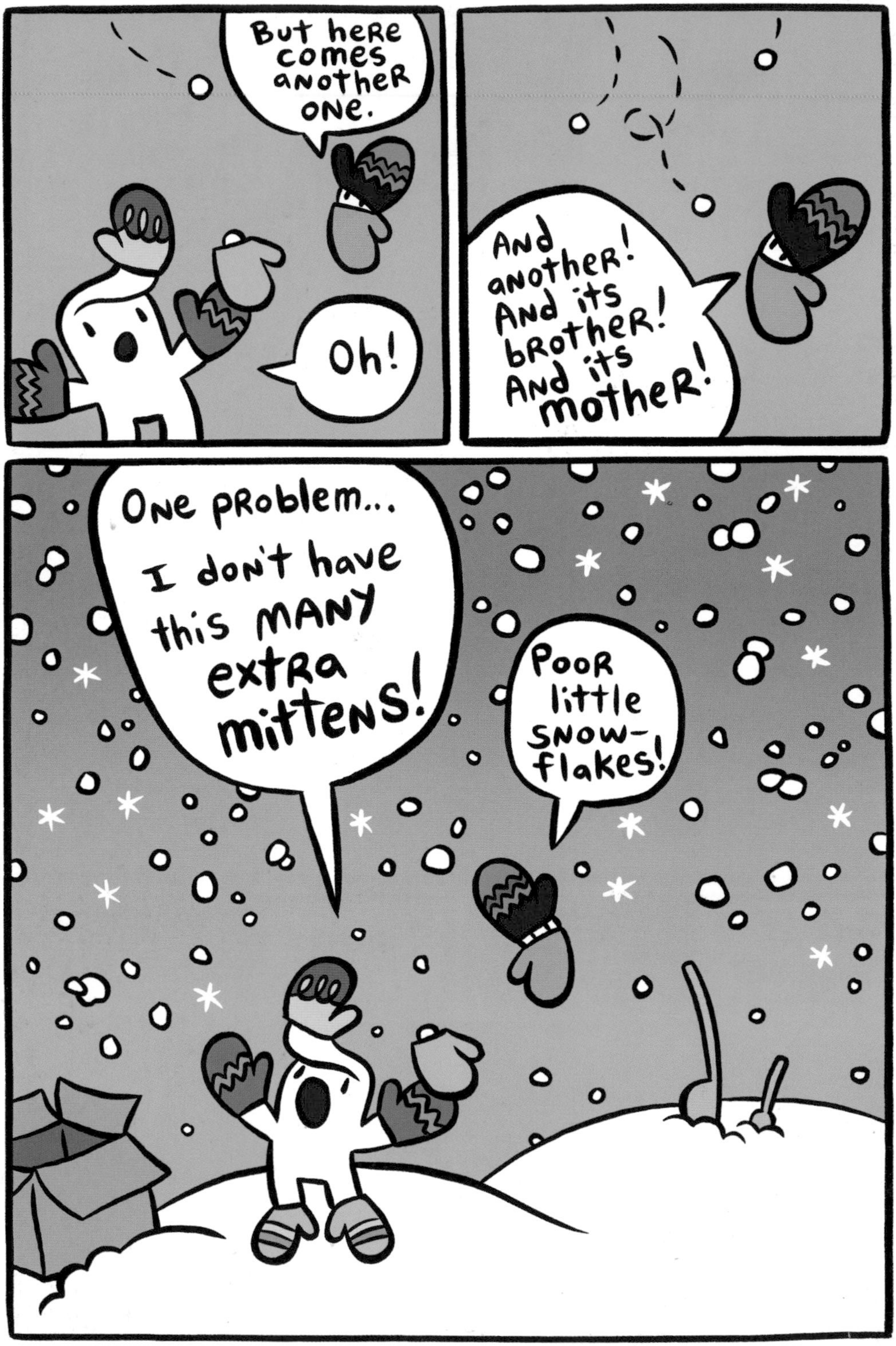
But here comes another one.
Oh!
And another! And its brother! And its mother!
One problem... I don't have this MANY extra mittens!
Poor little snow-flakes!

CHAPTER SIX

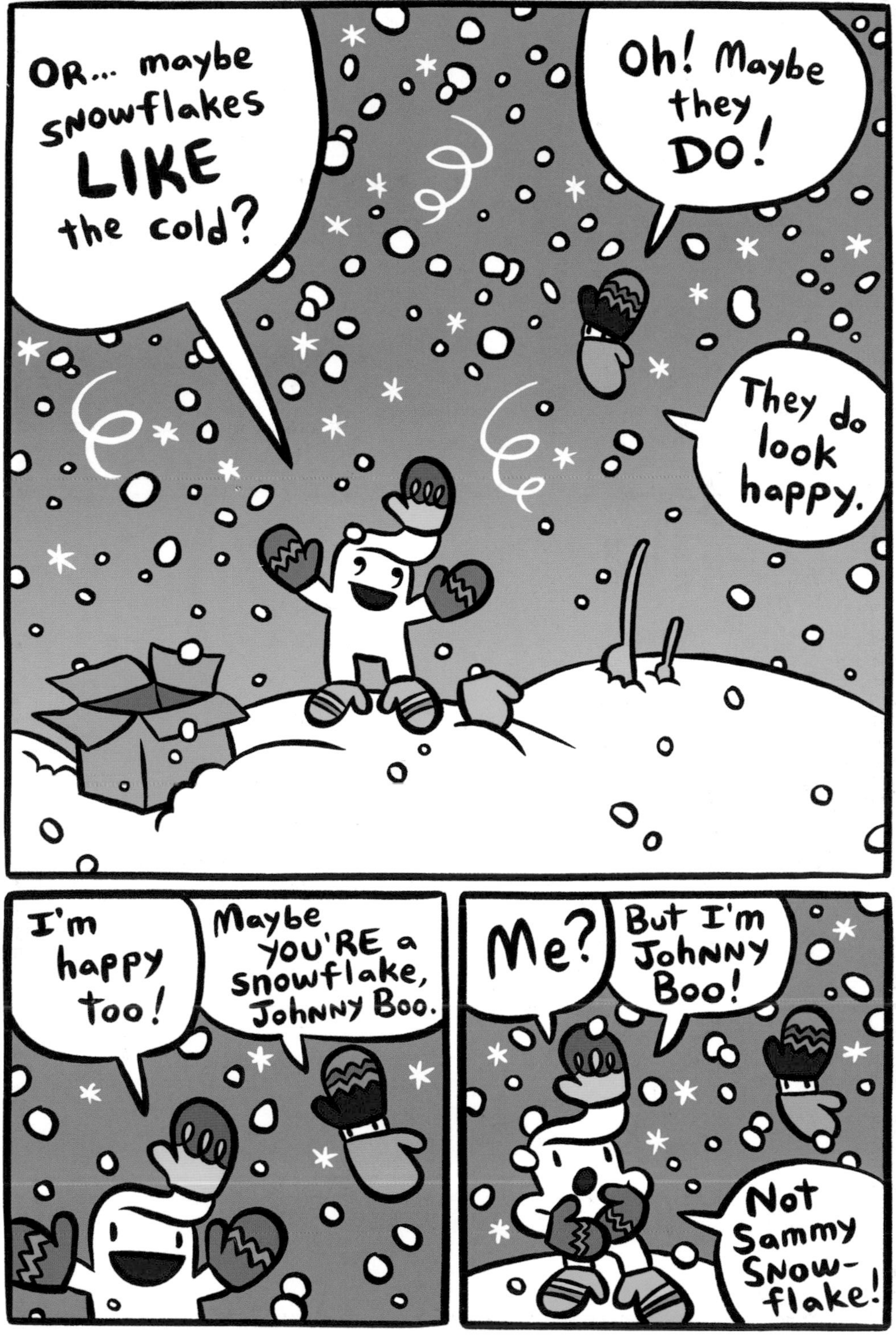
OR... maybe snowflakes LIKE the cold?
Oh! Maybe they DO!
They do look happy.
I'm happy too!
Maybe YOU'RE a snowflake, Johnny Boo.
Me?
But I'm Johnny Boo!
Not Sammy Snow-flake!

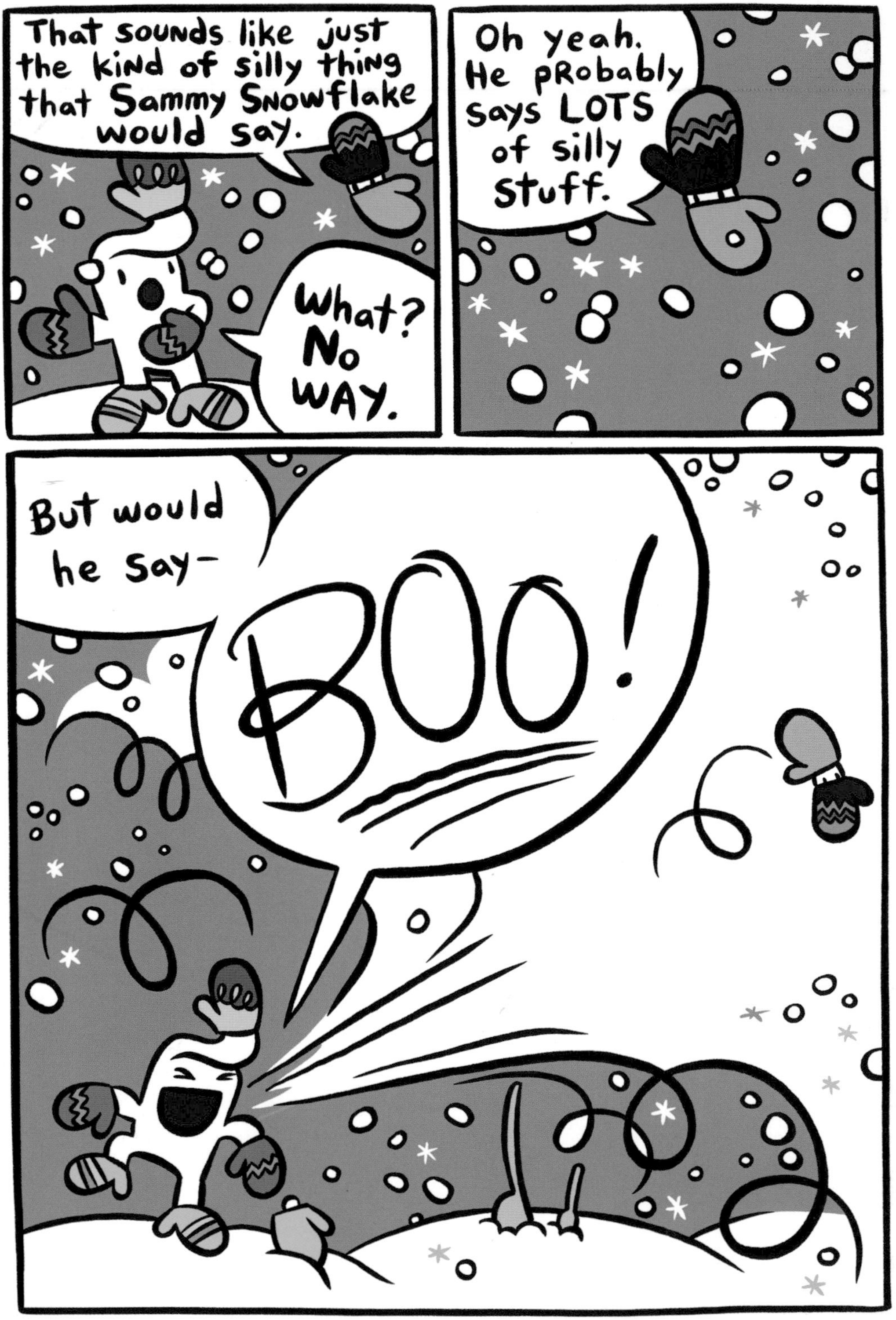
That sounds like just the kind of silly thing that Sammy Snowflake would say.
What? No WAY.
Oh yeah. He probably says LOTS of silly stuff.
But would he say-
BOO!

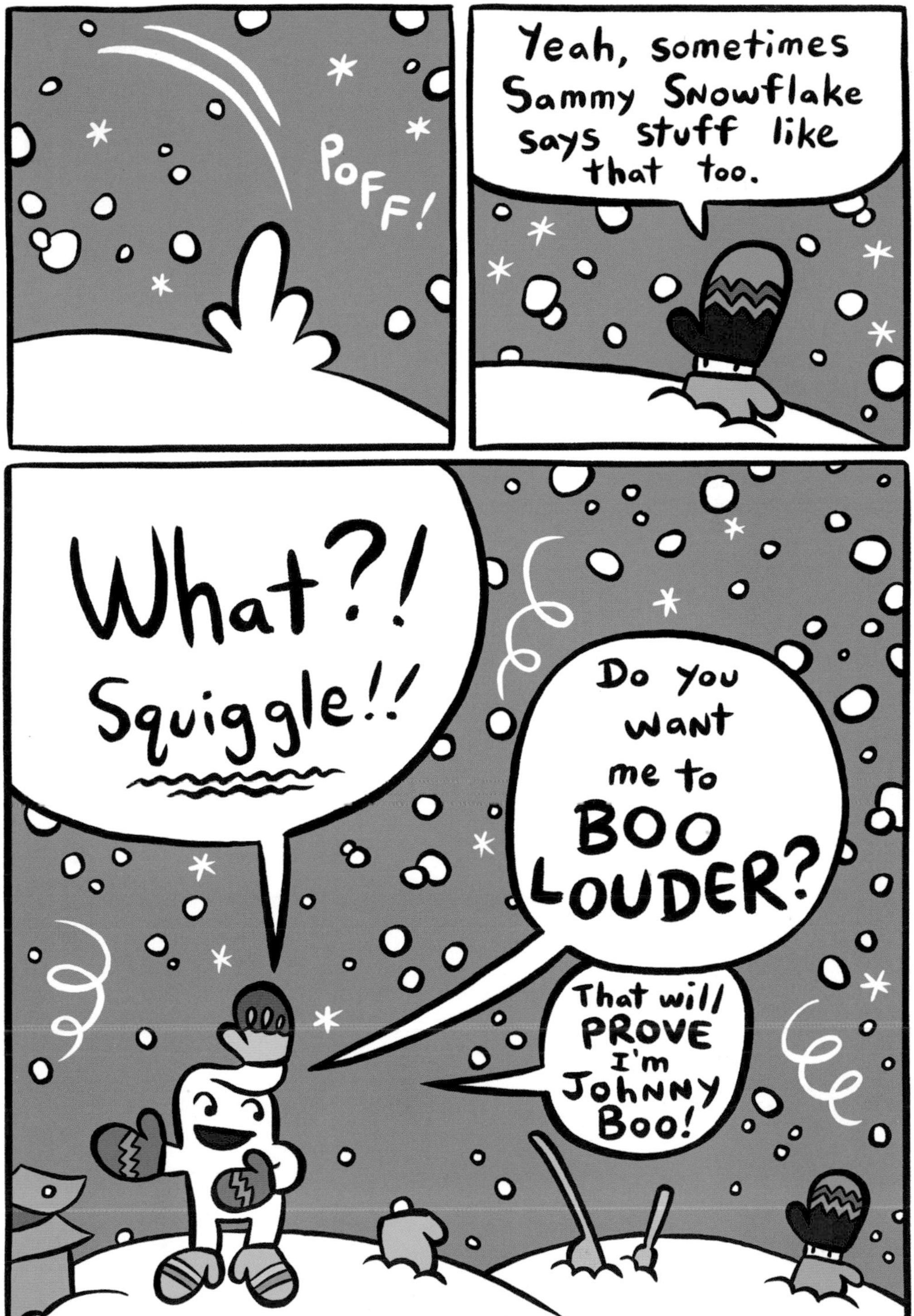
POFF!
Yeah, sometimes Sammy Snowflake says stuff like that too.
What?! Squiggle!!
Do you want me to BOO LOUDER?
That will PROVE I'm JOHNNY BOO!

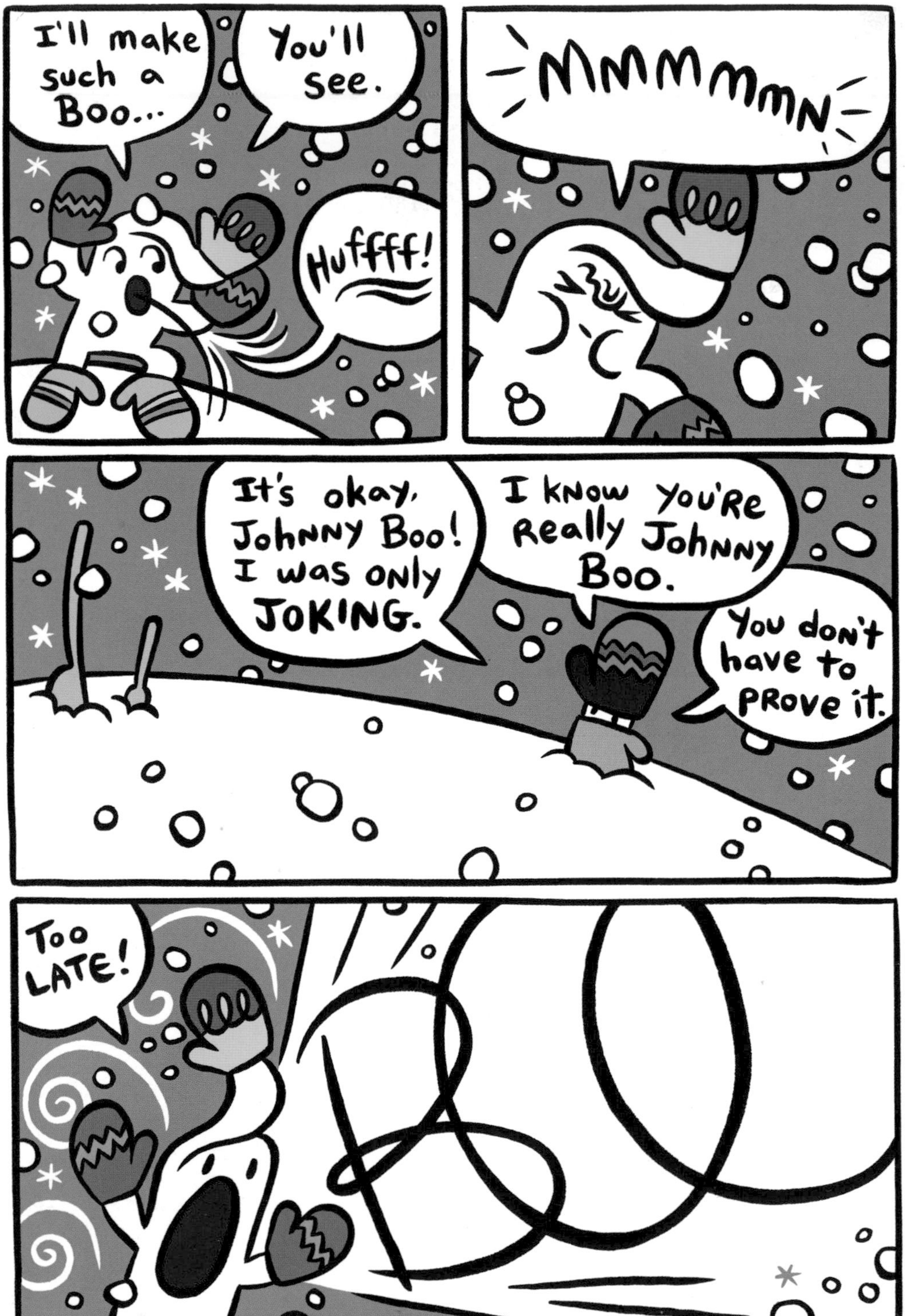
I'll make such a Boo...
You'll see.
Hufff!
MMMMMMN
It's okay, Johnny Boo! I was only JOKING.
I know you're really Johnny Boo.
You don't have to prove it.
Too LATE!

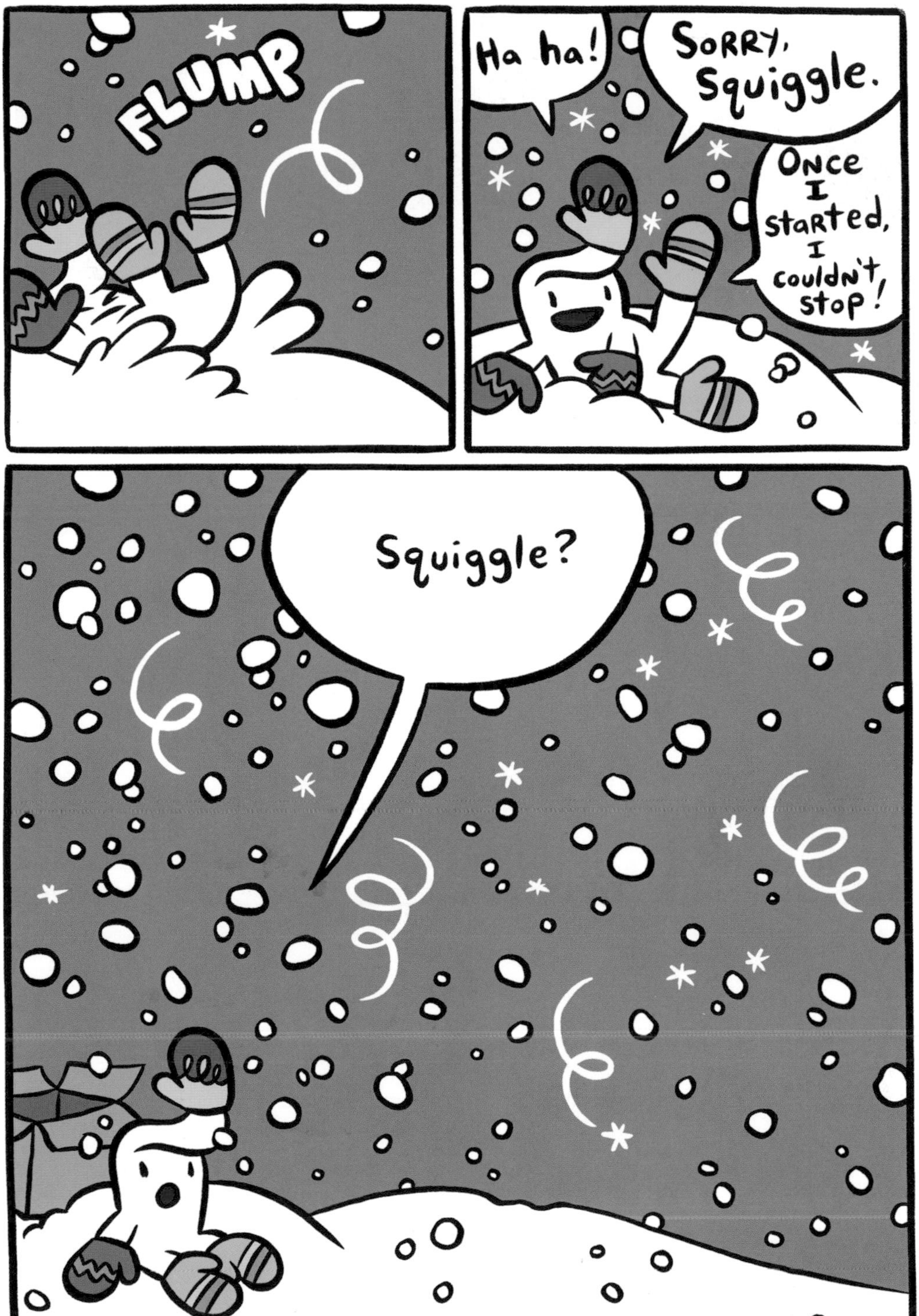
FLUMP
Ha ha!
SORRY, Squiggle.
Once I started, I couldn't stop!
Squiggle?

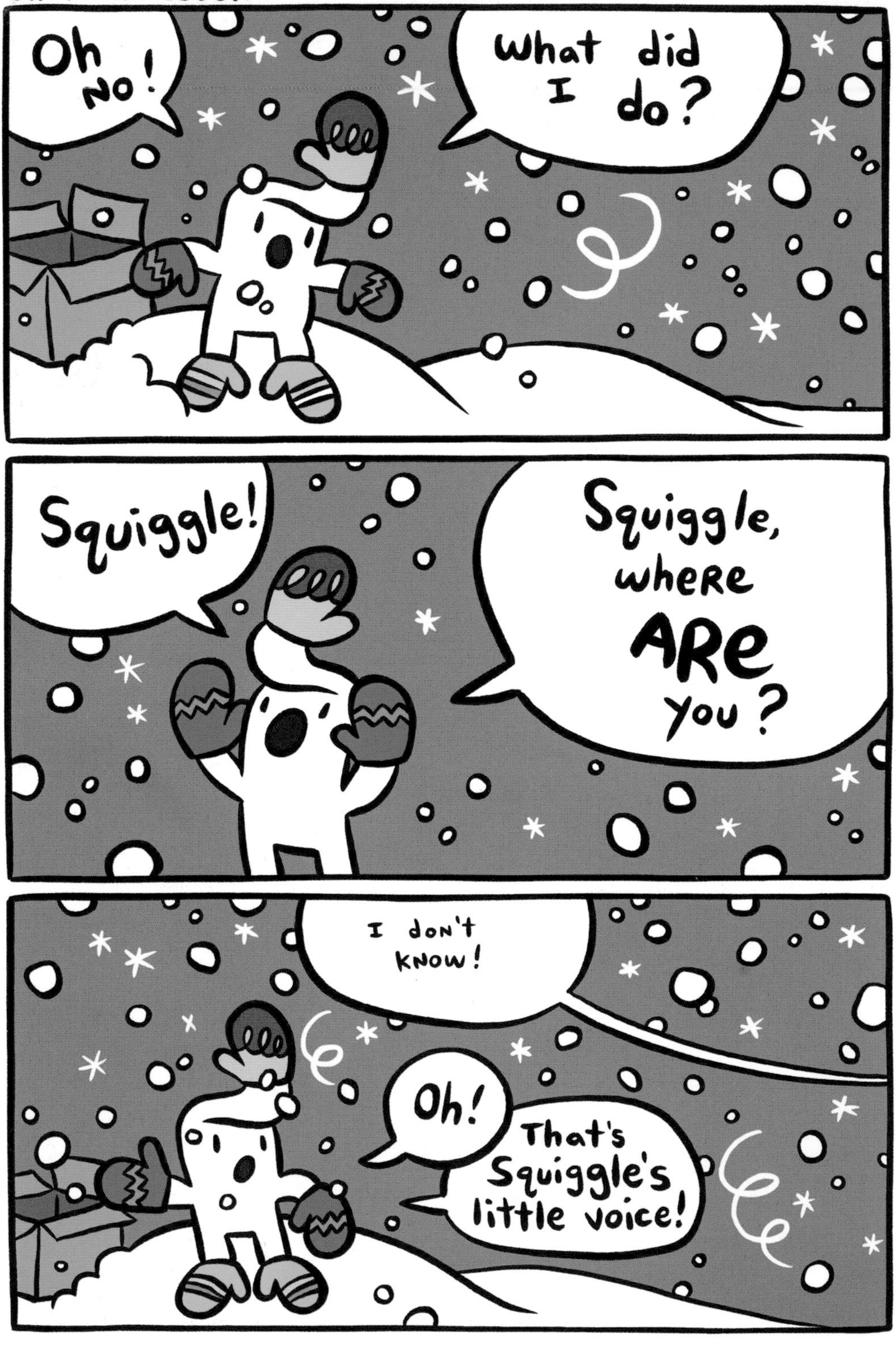
Oh NO!
What did I do?
Squiggle!
Squiggle, where ARE you?
I don't KNOW!
Oh!
That's Squiggle's little voice!

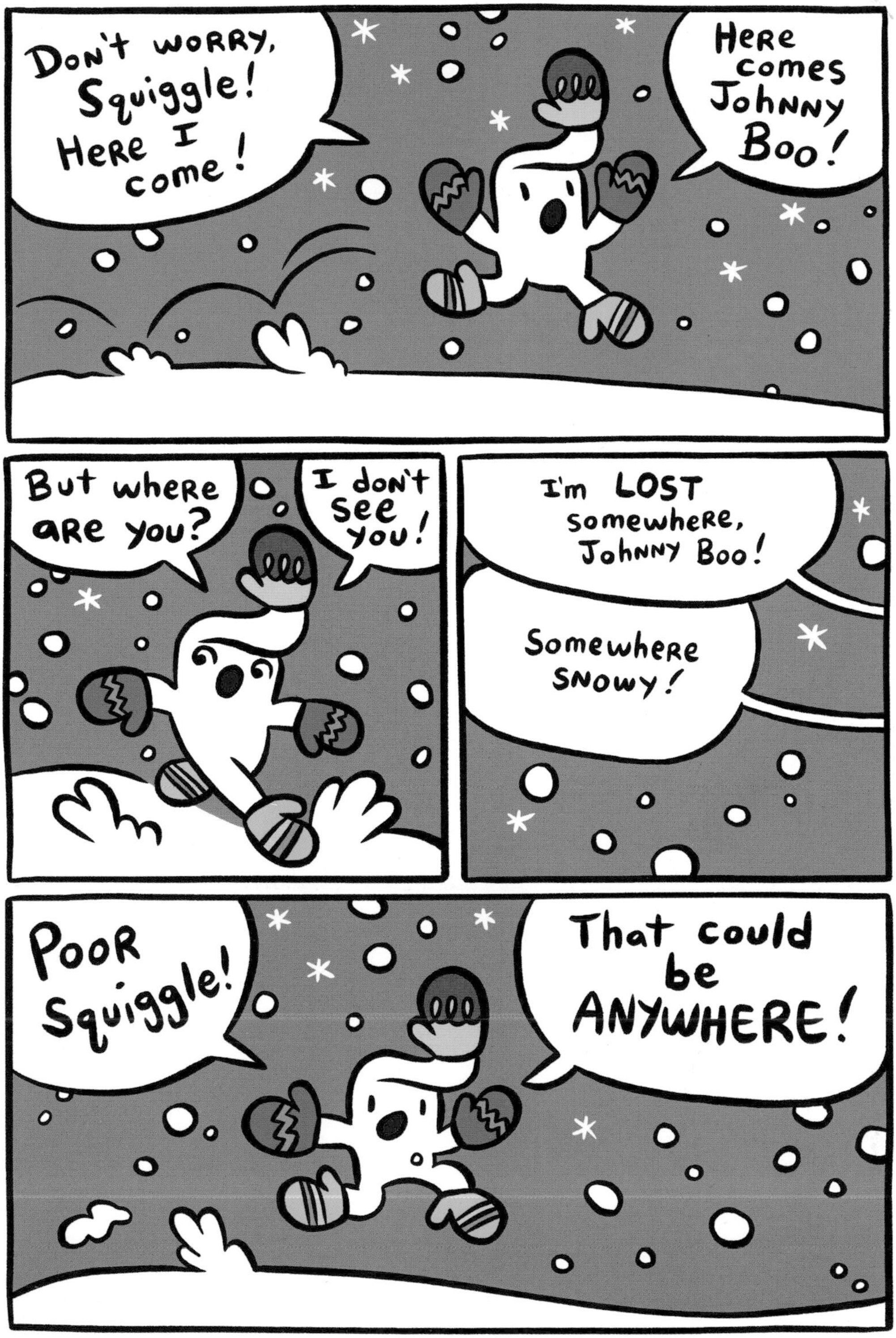
Don't worry, Squiggle! Here I come!
Here comes Johnny Boo!
But where are you?
I don't see you!
I'm LOST somewhere, Johnny Boo!
Somewhere snowy!
Poor Squiggle!
That could be ANYWHERE!

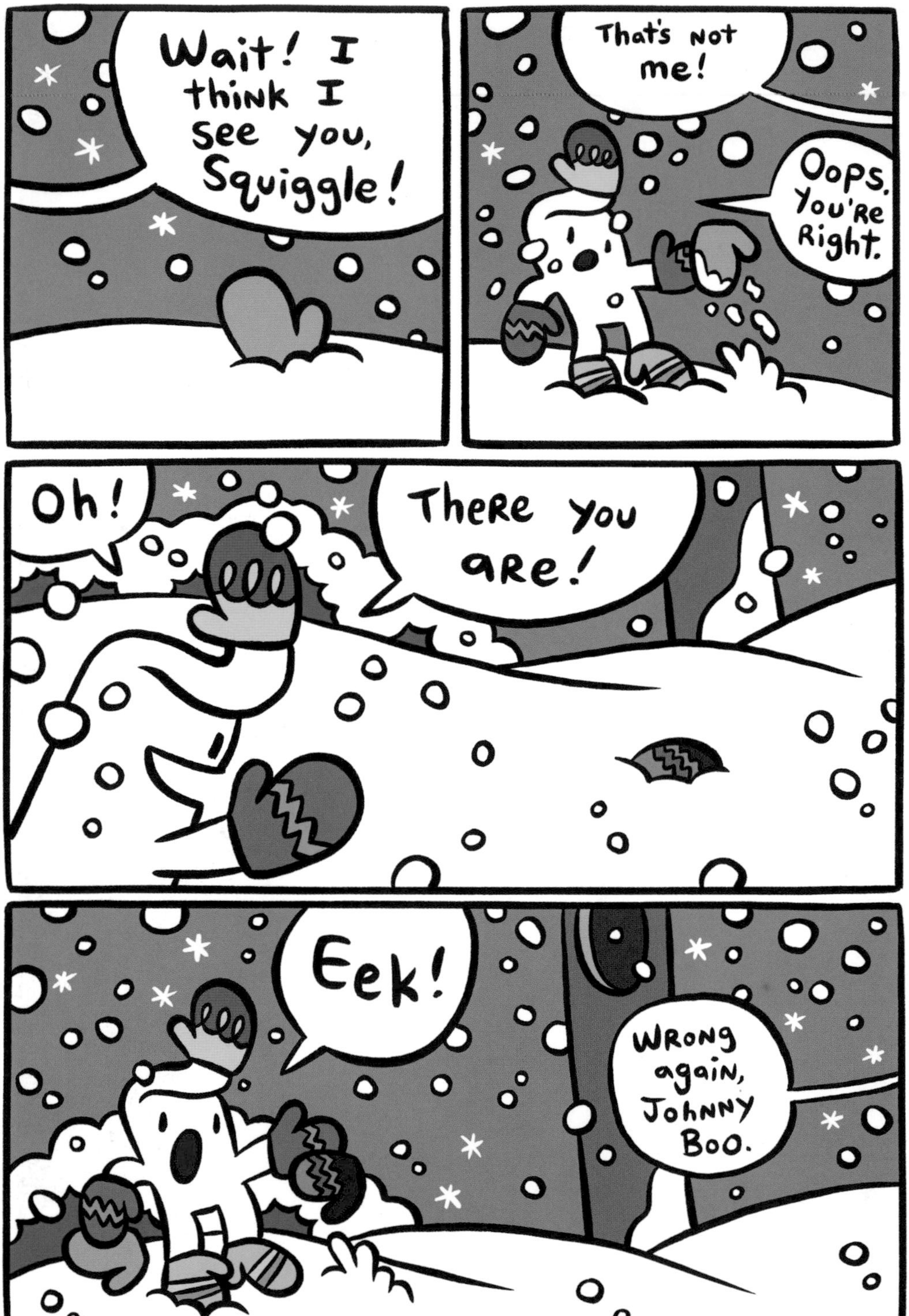
Wait! I think I see you, Squiggle!
That's not me!
Oops. You're Right.
Oh!
There you are!
Eek!
Wrong again, Johnny Boo.

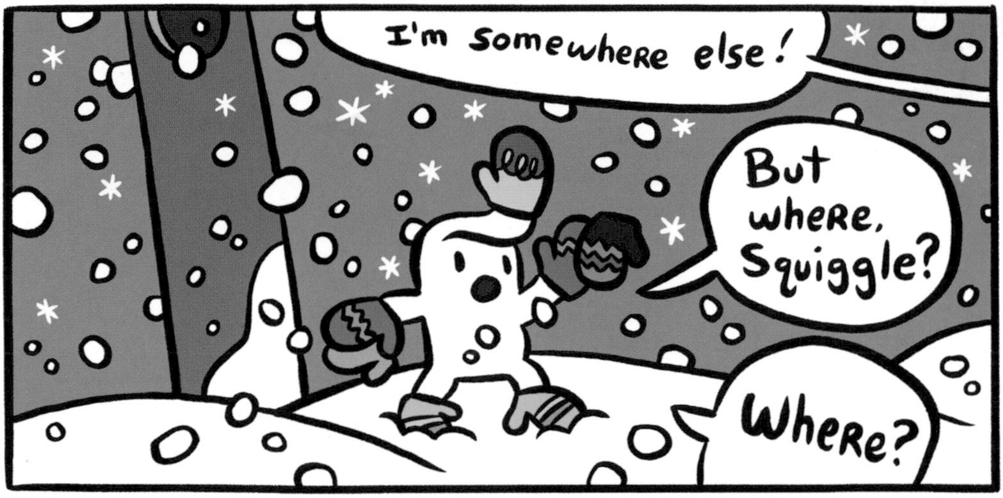
I'm somewhere else!
But where, Squiggle?
Where?

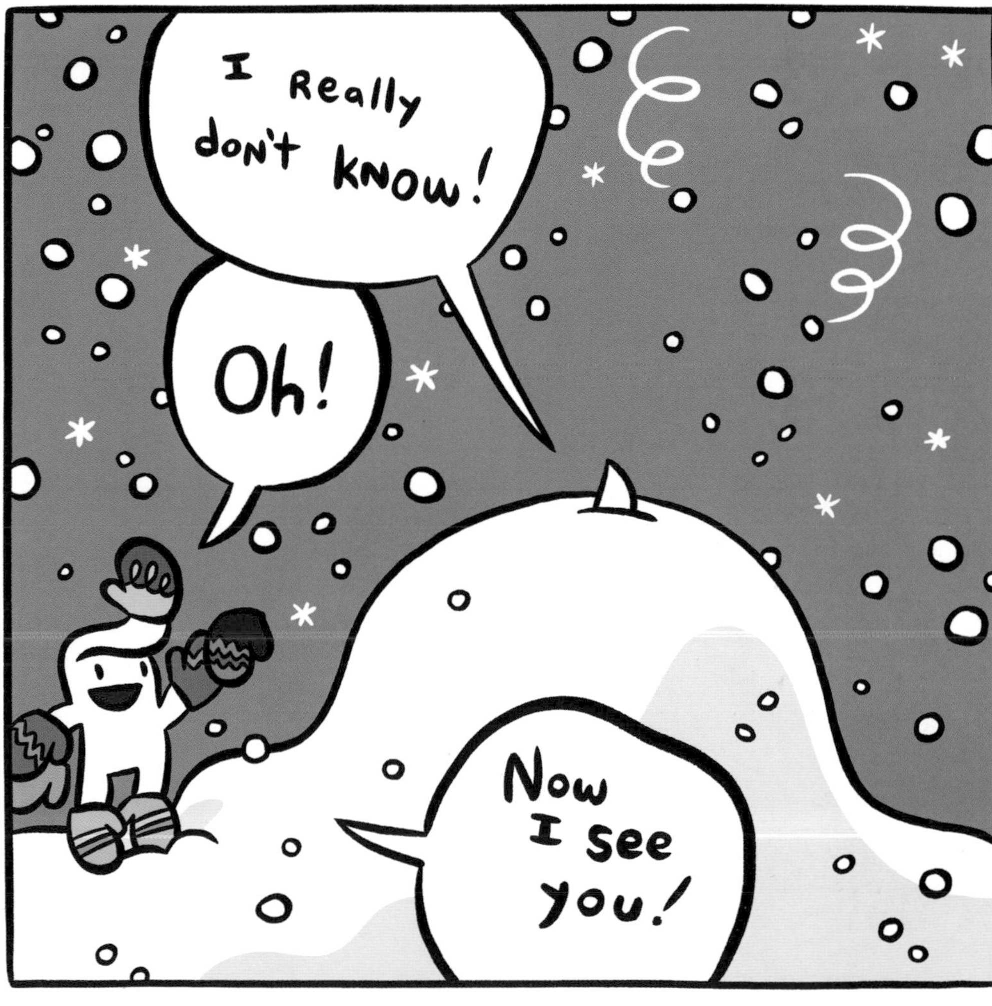
I really don't know!
Oh!
Now I see you!

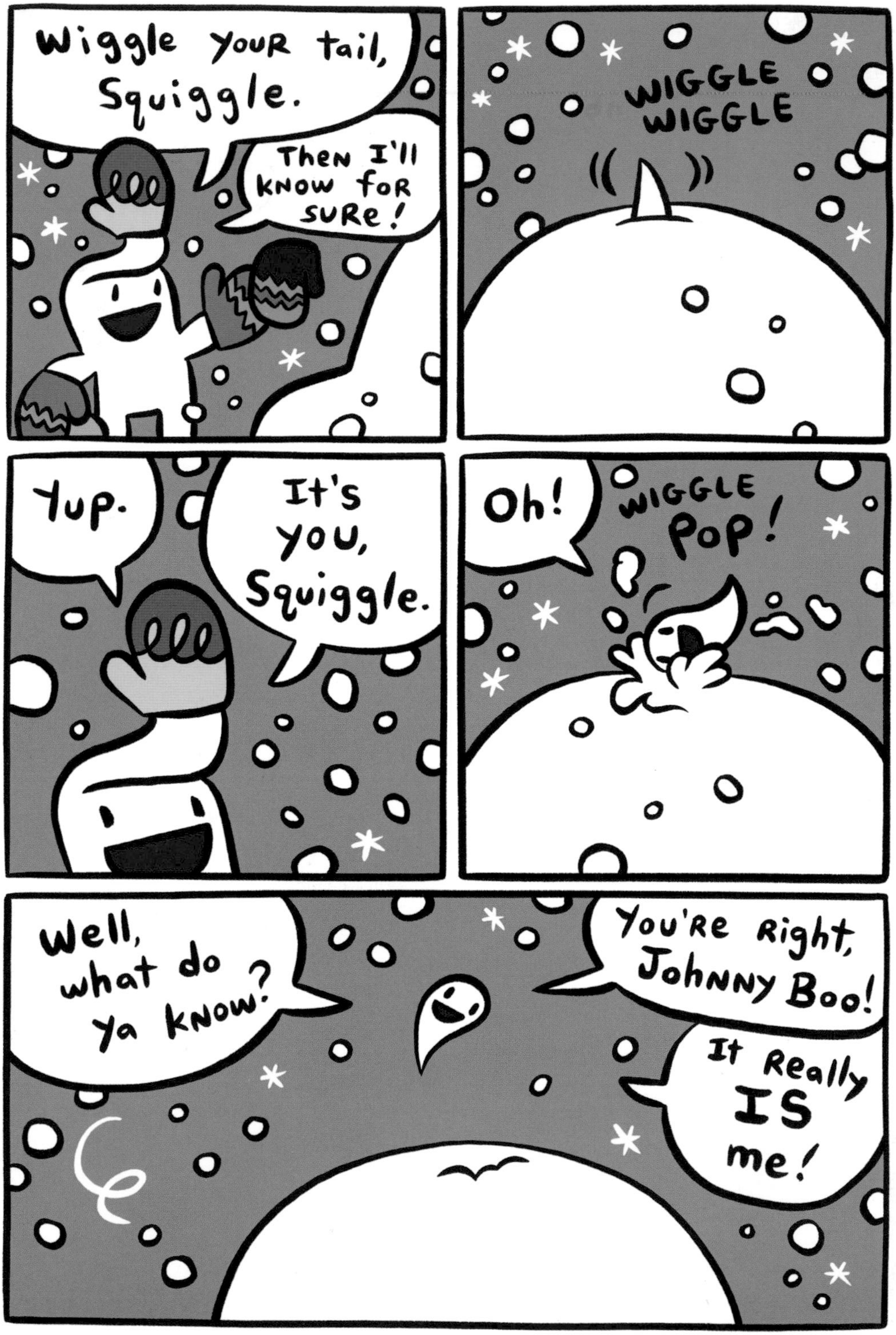
Wiggle your tail, Squiggle.
Then I'll know for sure!
WIGGLE WIGGLE
Yup.
It's you, Squiggle.
Oh!
WIGGLE POP!
Well, what do ya know?
You're right, Johnny Boo!
It really IS me!

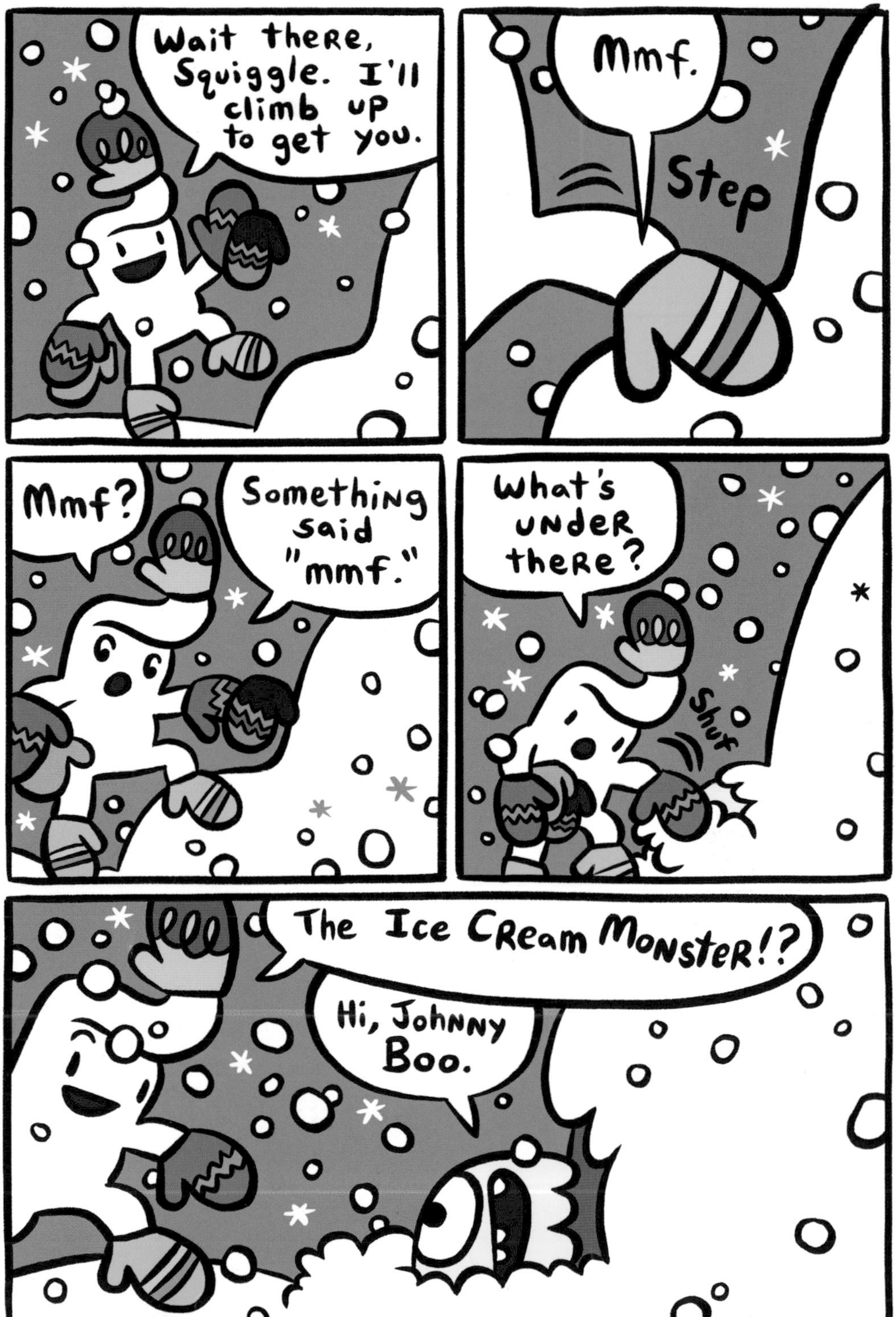

Wait there, Squiggle. I'll climb up to get you.
Mmf.
Step
Mmf?
Something said "mmf."
What's under there?
Shuf
The Ice Cream Monster!?
Hi, Johnny Boo.

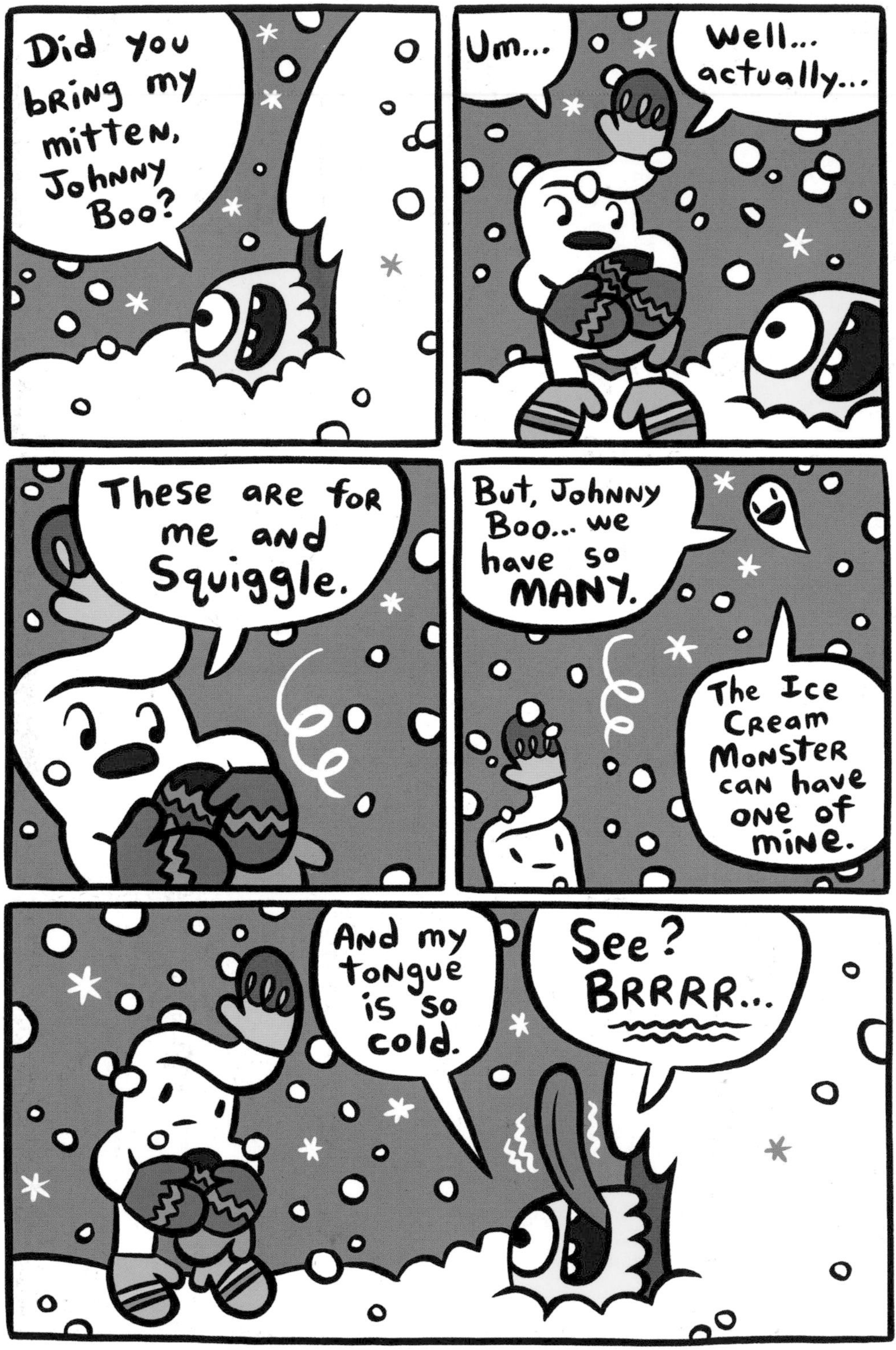
Did you bring my mitten, Johnny Boo?
Um...
Well... actually...
These are for me and Squiggle.
But, Johnny Boo... we have so MANY.
The Ice Cream Monster can have one of mine.
And my tongue is so cold.
See? BRRRR...

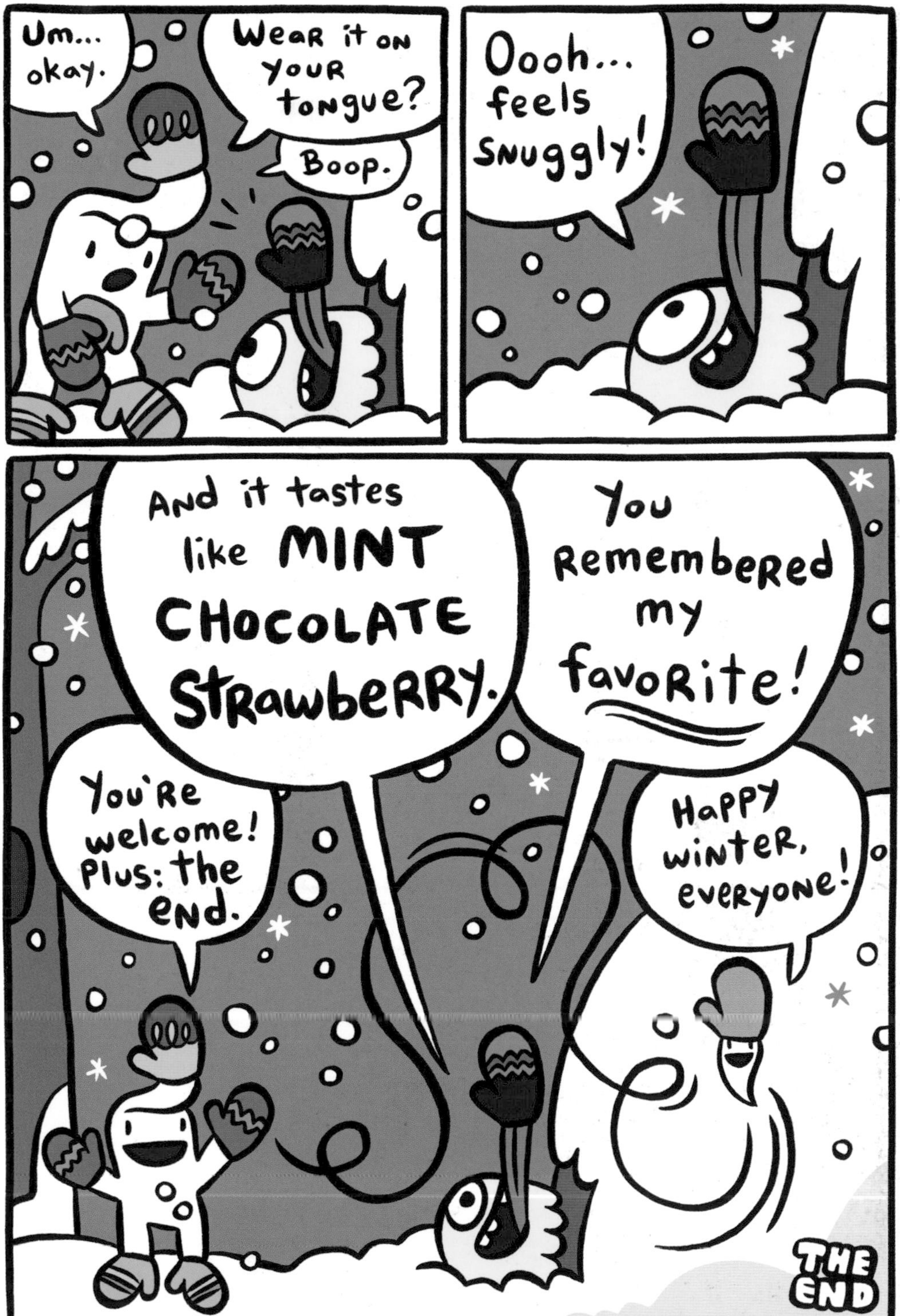
Um... okay.
Wear it on your tongue?
Boop.
Oooh... feels snuggly!
And it tastes like MINT CHOCOLATE STRAWBERRY.
You remembered my favorite!
You're welcome! Plus: the end.
Happy winter, everyone!
THE END

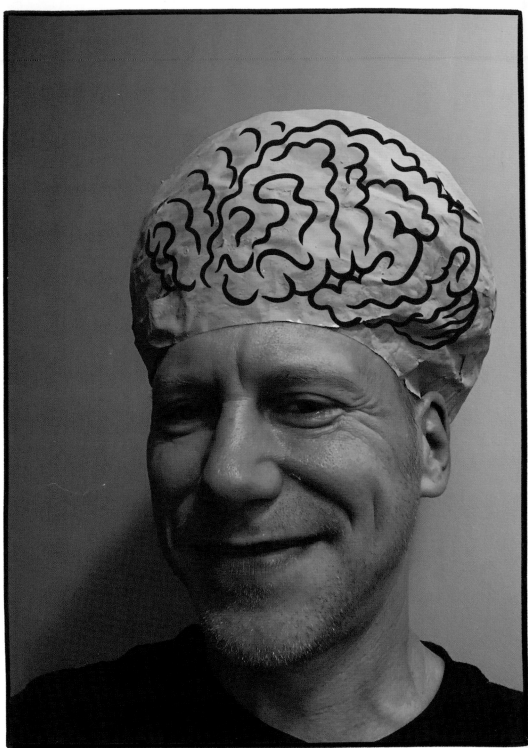

JAMES KOCHALKA USES HIS MASSIVE CARTOONIST BRAIN TO THINK UP NEW STORIES ABOUT JOHNNY BOO.